Little Lou's Sayings And Doings
By Elizabeth Prentiss

Updated for the modern reader
by Rebecca Perkins

Words, expressions and sentence structure have been
revised for better readability
and clarity.

Illustrations by Giselle A. Imperio

Copyright © 2014 for new content and illustrations.
R. Perkins, G. Imperio
All rights reserved.

Permission granted to reproduce small portions for personal and non-profit Sunday School use only. This material may not be duplicated for any profit-driven enterprise.

Scripture taken from the New King James Version®, unless otherwise noted. Copyright © 1982 by Thomas Nelson, Inc. Used by permission. All rights reserved.

Some Scripture taken from the Holy Bible, NEW INTERNATIONAL VERSION®. Copyright © 1973, 1978, 1984 by Biblica, Inc. All rights reserved worldwide. Used by permission.

ISBN: 978-09854708-6-9
United States of America

More Love Enterprises
Renewing Vintage Favorites

Forward

The following is an excerpt from the 1868 London Daily News: "*Little Lou is one of the most natural stories in the world, and reads more like a mother's record of her child's sayings and doings than like a fictitious narrative. Little Lou, be it remarked, is a true baby throughout, instead of being a precocious little prig, as so many good children are in print. The child's love for his mother and his mother's love for him are described in the prettiest way possible.*"

Elizabeth Prentiss' husband, Reverend George Prentiss, explained a little of the story's history: "*She devoted herself during the following weeks to the care of her little nephew [Eddy Hopkins]. Her letters written at the time —some of them with him in her arms—are full of his pretty ways; and when, more than a score of years later, he had given his young life to his country [in the Civil War] and was sleeping in a soldier's grave, his "sayings and doings" formed the subject of one of her most attractive juvenile books.*"

Introduction

As we continue our mission of modernizing vintage favorites, we are very excited to offer you *Little Lou's Sayings and Doings!* Parents often wish they had written down all the funny and poignant little things their children said, but for most of us, before we know it, time has passed and we've forgotten those precious words. This book is a look into the past through Elisabeth Prentiss's journal, where she lovingly recorded details of her nephew's life. I can just see the twinkle in her eye as she chuckled and wrote down something he said to be sure she would not forget it. You will enjoy many hours with your children reading this delightful story, and I hope this book inspires you to record their precious comments so that they too can have memories like this. *Little Lou* is my favorite Elisabeth Prentiss children's book.

Rebecca Perkins
July 2014

Little Lou's

Sayings and Doings

Part 1

Chapter 1

Little Lou was six months old. He was born when the flowers were blooming and all the birds were singing. It was long ago when there were no cars or TVs or video games. Cold winter had come now and killed the flowers and driven away the birds, but it couldn't kill Lou or drive him away. He lay warm and happy in his mama's arms and didn't know how cold it was outside. How his mama loved him! She so wished his grandma and his four uncles and his Aunt Samantha could see him! Don't *you* always want your mother to see every present you have? But you never had a real live baby as a present to show her.

Every time Lou laughed, cooed, and clapped his hands, his mother longed to have everybody in her old home see what a little darling he was. One day he was dressed in a cute outfit that his grandma had sent him and his eyes danced and sparkled as his mama swung him up and down. She thought he looked like a little cherub. She said to his papa, "I *really* want my mother to see Lou."

"It would be quite a long trip to take with such a little baby," said his papa. "But he wouldn't be out in the cold if we took the train."

"And the rest of the way he could be bundled up in warm clothes and blankets," said his mama. So after a little more talk about it, Lou's papa decided that they would all go to Grandma's house the next week. Then his mama kissed Little Lou over and over and told him all about it. Though he didn't understand a word she said, he knew by her joyful face that she was talking about something nice, and he laughed until his eyes sparkled with fun.

Now it was time to pack the trunks and get ready for the journey. All of Lou's clothes were checked to see if they were ready to go. Some of them had to be washed and ironed, and there were so many other things to do that everybody was busy and the whole house was in an uproar.

"Now Lou," said Mama, "I hope you'll take a long nap today, to give me time to get everything ready for our trip. Oh my! There is so much to do! I hardly know where to begin!" Papa said he would pack everything in half an hour, and he picked up a pile of clean, neatly folded shirts, and rolled them up in a tight little roll, and squeezed them down into one corner of the trunk. Mama shrieked.

"You're crushing and wrinkling the baby's best things!" she cried. Oh William, how *could* you!" Papa looked a little frightened.

"I don't know much about clothes," he said, "but give me something else. What are all these bottles for? Are you going to bring milk for Lou?"

"Men never know what's going on with packing!" cried Mama, laughing. "I'm going to take some currant jelly to mother and some strawberry jelly to Sammy. Sammy loves strawberry jelly. And for the boys, I have a few bottles of raspberry vinegar, that's all. I don't care how tightly you pack them up, the tighter the better!"

Chapter 2

It was a cold evening and Grandma, who had been sitting by the fire knitting and reading, finally let her book fall from her lap. She had fallen asleep in her chair. The four uncles sat around the table, two of them playing chess, and two watching. Aunt Samantha, who everyone called Sammy, sat with her cat on her knees and studied French a little. She looked at the clock every few minutes and jumped at every noise. "I've said all along that they wouldn't come," she cried at last. "It's 9 o'clock, and I'm not going to wait for them anymore. I knew William wouldn't let Laura take such a long trip in the middle of winter! Or Laura would change her mind at the last minute."

She had hardly finished saying this when the doorbell rang. Then there were feet stamping on the mat to shake off the snow, and in they came: Lou, and Lou's papa and mama, bringing all the fresh, cold air with them. Grandma woke up and ran to meet them, running as quickly as if she were a young girl. Aunt Sammy tossed the cat from her lap and seized the bundle of baby. The four uncles crowded about her, eager to get the first peek at the little wonder. There was such laughing and commotion that poor Lou, coming out of the dark night into the bright room, and seeing so many strange faces, didn't know what to think. When his coats and blankets and hat were finally pulled off by his auntie's eager hands, there appeared a serious little face, a pair of bright eyes, and a head as smooth as ivory. He didn't have a single hair. His sleeves were folded up and showed his plump white arms and he sat up very straight and took a good look at everybody.

"What a perfect little face!" "What beautiful eyes!" "What lovely skin!" "He's the perfect image of his father!" "He's *exactly* like his mother!" "What a cute little nose!" "What fat little hands full of dimples!" "Let *me* take him!" "Come to your Grandma!" "Let his uncle toss him!" "What does he eat?" "Is he hungry?" "Was he good on his trip?" "Is he tired?" "Now *Sammy!* You've had him ever since he came. He wants to come to me, I know he does!"

These, and I don't know how many more exclamations like them greeted the ears of the little stranger and he heard them without even smiling. "The poor child is scared out of his wits," said his mama, who had been laughing until she cried. "I really should undress him and put him to bed."

Immediately everybody had something to do in the best room upstairs. Grandma wanted to see that the little crib was ready. Aunt Sammy was sure there weren't enough towels on the rack. Uncle Robert said the baby was too heavy to be carried up in any arms but his own. Uncle Tom declared that the fire must be getting low, and the two others followed with carpetbags, coats and umbrellas.

"What an important person I am these days!" cried the young mama. "The whole family waiting on me! Maybe some of you would like to rock *me* to sleep!" There was more laughing and commotion, but at last she got everybody out of the room. There was a great creaking of boots on the stairs, and the sound of people telling each other to "Hush!" in loud whispers, and at last all was quiet.

Chapter 3

The next morning Lou awoke quite rested and full of fun, and before his mama was dressed, Aunt Sammy came and knocked at the door.

"Well?" said Mama.

"I wanted to know," called Aunt Sammy through the door, "if Baby is awake, and if I can take him downstairs. The boys are dying to see him in the daylight."

"I can't believe this!" said Mama to herself. She opened the door a little bit and handed Lou out. Aunt Sammy seized him and ran happily downstairs.

"I've got him," she cried, running into the dining room. "I've got him! And he's the nicest, best and cutest baby in the world!"

"Let me have him, Sammy, please," said Uncle Robert. "I have to leave right after breakfast and you can have him all day."

"I'm leaving before Bob," cried Uncle Tom, "and I've barely seen him yet." Aunt Sammy pressed the baby to her heart, covering him with kisses and singing "Rock-a-by-Baby" loudly.

"How silly you are, Sammy," said Uncle Frank. "Trying to get the baby to sleep as soon as he's up in the morning. Just give me one good look at him! Yes, he *is* a handsome boy. No wonder you all say he looks just like me." Then he grabbed Lou from Sammy's arms, and escaped with him from the room. Once out of sight of them all, he too started kissing the little baby so much that it's a good thing there is no such thing as being loved to death!

By the time breakfast was ready, everybody had held the little guy. He had been taken to the kitchen and showed off to Mary and Martha, and made to pet Uncle Fred's dog with his little hand and feel Aunt Sammy's cat. Kitty, however, pretended that she didn't like him at all. When Sammy, who always loved her and never read or studied without her pet in her lap, had tossed her away in order to hold the baby, Kitty's feelings were deeply hurt. "*Ha!*" she said to herself, "*I won't go into the living room again while that child is here. I'm not going to sit on the floor and see that strange boy up in my place! Not on your life!*" So, the whole six weeks that Lou stayed at his grandma's, Miss Kitty pouted in the kitchen and never set foot in the living room until the day he left. Then she was in a good mood again, and went back to Sammy's lap as if nothing had happened.

After breakfast Lou's uncles all went away to their offices and their businesses, Grandma went to the kitchen to talk with Mary, and Papa went out to take a long walk over the packed down snow. Mama could now wash and dress her baby in peace, while Aunt Sammy looked on with wonder and curiosity.

"I suppose there is no cradle in the house," said Mama as she buttoned Lou's shirt and held him up for Sammy to look at him in his fresh, clean clothes.

"No, sorry. Ours was given to Jane—you remember our old friend Jane? Well, it was given to Jane's daughter, when her first baby was born.

"I don't know where Lou will take his naps," said his mama. "I'll want to be where the rest of you are, but I don't feel it's safe to leave him alone."

"I can stay with him," said Aunt Sammy.

"Oh, but I'll want you to be where I am. I have at least five hundred things to talk about. Besides, I want Lou to keep up the habit of sleeping where everything is going on as usual. At home I keep the cradle in the room where I sit with my books or my work. William is constantly coming in and out, and never closes the door quietly. So I've trained Lou to sleep through everything."

Chapter 4

WHILE THE SISTERS were talking, Lou had fallen fast asleep, lulled by the sound of voices, and comforted with a warm breakfast that he had been getting for himself. His head sank gradually back on his mama's arm, his little fingers let go of their hold on one of her curls he had been playing with, and his mouth half opened like a bud that will soon be a red rose.

"He's the most beautiful baby I've ever seen!" cried Aunt Sammy. "Laura, why didn't you ever tell us what a beauty he was? All you said was that he had a bald head, and I never liked bald-headed babies."

"I really didn't know whether he was beautiful or not," replied his mama. "I knew he had very beautiful eyes, but all mothers think their babies are beautiful. I didn't know if everyone else would, too." Just then Grandma came smiling into the room, followed on tiptoe by three little girls who gathered around the baby with delighted faces, but as quietly as three little mothers.

"These are Mrs. Redwood's little girls," said Grandma. "They have brought their doll's bed for Lou to take his naps in."

"Their doll's bed!" repeated Lou's mama, smiling.

"Our dolly is a great big dolly, as big as a real live baby!" whispered Josephine, the oldest. "And mama said it would be very—very—"

"Very convenient," put in her sister Jeanie.

"Very convenient for our dolly to lie on the bed in our guest room, while your little baby was here."

"No, she said it would be convenient to you to use our dolly's bed," corrected Jeanie.

"And our dolly don't care where she sleeps, not a bit," said little Hattie.

"But is your doll bed really big enough for Lou?" asked his mother. "Look what a big boy he is."

"Our dolly is a great big dolly, as big as a real live baby!" repeated Josephine.

"Yes, she is a great big dolly, as big as a real live baby," said both of the others sisters.

"It's a very sturdy little bed and it will be fine for Lou," said Grandma. "I've made room for it in a corner of my room, and you can all come and see how well our baby will fit into it."

Sure enough, the bed with its soft linen sheets, little pillow, and pretty white quilt seemed to have been made just for Lou. When his mama had gently laid him down in it, the three little girls tenderly pulled the blankets over him, tucked them in with skillful hands, and stood admiring their work like three adorable little mothers.

"Thank you, girls. You're very kind to lend your dolly's bed to my baby," said Lou's mama. "I hope your dolly won't miss it very much. Do you think she wanted to let us use it?"

"She never said a word when she heard us talking about it," cried little Jeanie. "She isn't a shellfish dolly at all. But I know a shellfish girl, I do."

"I ain't a shellfish," cried Hattie, bursting into tears. "I only said—I only said—I only said dolly would be lonely away off in the guest room, without her own bed and without any fire." Lou's mama

15

stood thinking a moment, and then went quickly to her own room and came running back with three little books in her hands.

"I stopped in Boston long enough to buy some books," she said. "And here is one for each of you. Look! They're full of pictures. Look, Hattie. When your dolly gets lonely, you can pick her up and show her these pictures."

"Yes, I can," said Hattie, her tearful face lighting up. "I sure can."

When the three little girls were on the sidewalk on their way home, Josephine said to Jeanie, "You shouldn't have said that about Hattie. Mama she said wasn't selfish at all. She said she was tender-hearted, and couldn't bear to think that dolly might suffer."

"Dolly can't suffer!" cried Jeanie. "She isn't a real baby. She's nothing but a make-believe baby. I'm going to stick a pin in her as soon as I get home and it won't hurt her one bit. And now that I've seen a real live baby, I don't like dolly anymore. Mrs. James's baby is soft and warm. It can breathe and it can eat. But dolly is as hard as a rock and she feels cold and she can't go to sleep. She just pretends she's a baby, when she ain't."

Chapter 5

WHILE LOU WAS enjoying his nap, his mama took all his little nightgowns and clothes from the trunk and arranged them in the drawers of the dresser. Aunt Sammy helped her and admired all the cute things.

"How beautifully you sew!" she said. "I never saw such nice stitches! I can't imagine when you found time to make so many things." Lou's mama laughed.

"I can't either," she said. "William used to wonder why I made so many. He said he would think 'one set of clothes' was enough for such a little baby."

"Men sure are funny!" said Aunt Sammy. Grandma came in now.

"I hope you're almost ready to come and sit down, dear," she said. "The baby is sleeping sweetly and we can have a nice chat."

"I guess I can leave the rest of the unpacking awhile," said Lou's mama. "Oh, here are the bottles and things down in the bottom of the trunk. Look, Mom, I've brought you some of my own currant jelly. We have loads of currants, and when I was making my jelly, it was just as easy to make enough for you."

"Thank you, honey," said Grandma. "I'm always glad to have currant jelly!"

"The strawberry jelly is for Sammy, and the raspberry vinegar is for the boys."

"You have strawberries and raspberries in the garden, as well as currents?"

"Yes, we have all sorts of fruit. See, there are some good things about living in the country. And as for flowers…oh I wish you could see my flowers! William had a lot before I went there, and now we have more than we know what to do with." By this time everything was in order. Aunt Sammy had carried all the bottles to the pantry, Grandma had her knitting, and all three sat down in the room where Lou was sleeping.

"Is Lou as beautiful as you expected, Mother?" asked Lou's mama, while she fastened a bit of blue ribbon to a little white dress. In those days, baby boys wore dresses! "Do you think he looks like any of us did when we were babies? And which is he most like, his father or me?"

Grandma took off her glasses and looked long and tenderly at the little sleeper. "He's not like any of my children," she said. "They all had hair. And I don't see that he is like his father or like you. But he is a beautiful baby, and full of life and spirit."

"Oh, you can't imagine how full of life he is when he's himself. He's shy here, among so many strangers. The boys will really enjoy him when he starts to laugh and bounce, as he does at home."

Maybe you think it is a little funny that Lou's mama always spoke of her brothers as "the boys" since they were all grownups and had whiskers and went to jobs. But they hadn't always been men. They used to be boys, and Mama was so used to calling them that, that it was hard to call them anything else. On this day, about half an hour before dinner, they all came in, one after another.

"Robert, you're home early today!" cried Grandma.

"And here's Tom!" said Aunt Sammy.

"Frank and Fred are in, too," said Lou's dad. "I met them on the stairs as I came down."

"I hope you don't mind my being early, Mother," said Uncle Robert. He picked up little Lou, who was now wide-awake, and held him up over his head.

"Oh Robert! Be careful!" said Lou's mama.

"I wouldn't have hurried home if I had known Bob was coming," said Uncle Tom. "I thought *I* would have some fun with the baby before dinner. Look here, Sir! See what Uncle Tom has brought you!" and he held up an ivory rattle, with silver bells in front of the delighted baby.

"Hey! I bought him a rattle, too," said Uncle Frank. "Well, it doesn't matter. He can hold one in each hand. There you are! Rattle away, my little man." Lou took a rattle in each hand, and shook them with all his might. His eyes sparkled and his face was covered with smiles.

But now it was Uncle Robert's turn, who offered the baby a large, round orange. Instantly Lou dropped the rattles and seized the orange with both hands. Uncle Robert laughed, in great triumph. But Mama and Papa and Grandma and Aunt Sammy all cried out at the same time that the orange must be taken away from the baby, who had already found out that it was good to eat, and had made the print of his two white teeth in the peel. Baby was not at all happy when his papa pried open his little fingers and took the orange away. Everybody told him oranges were not good for babies, that oranges were bad, very bad, and made faces at it and shook their heads at it. But it didn't do any good because Lou thought he knew better than all of them put together, and he cried very hard and very loudly for a long time.

Chapter 6

In a few days Lou felt quite at home among his new friends. They all loved him so dearly, and were so happy when he was pleased, and so sorry when anything troubled him, that he couldn't help loving them. His mama used to say that she believed Grandma would give him her two eyes if he wanted them. Grandma herself she said loved him just as much as she used to love her own little boys and girls. She would sit and watch him while he slept, with her knitting in her hands and her Bible and hymnbook by her side. And as she looked at that innocent face, she prayed in her heart that it would never be ugly with anger, and that those little white hands might never be busy in any evil work.

His uncles were never tired of carrying him about in their arms or on their shoulders. Every day they brought him home some little toy or made new ones for him with their jackknives. At nine o'clock every night, his mama, who was not very strong, gave him a little supper and put him back into his tiny bed, and left him to Aunt Sammy's care while she went to bed. Uncle Frank and Aunt Sammy always sat up until twelve, to read and study together. Every time the baby stirred they both ran to see if anything was the matter, and cover him up or put more coals on the fire so he would be warm enough. At twelve he always awoke and thought he was very hungry. Then his young babysitters picked him up, fed him a little milk, and made him comfortable. When he fell asleep again, someone carried him on tiptoe to his mama's room and laid him in the crib by her side. Oh, what happy midnight watches those were!

So day after day, and week after week slipped by, until Lou's papa said his vacation was almost over, and it was time for them to go home. Again there was the packing of little white nightgowns and shirts. The rattles and other toys filled the places that the bottles had left empty, and the trunks declared they were so full they could hold no more. Even so, Grandma made them take in a big loaf of frosted cake, and a good many other little packages that she didn't tell mama about. The trunks were so full that Uncle Robert had to stand on both of them to keep the covers down while papa locked them.

Everybody felt sad about them leaving except Lou. When his hat and coat were put on, he began to laugh and coo and bounce, for he knew that meant that he was going somewhere, and he didn't care where as long as he was going somewhere. When the carriage came to the door to take them to the train, the four uncles pretended they were very happy because they didn't like to be seen crying. After Uncle Frank handed Lou in to his mama, all bundled up as he was, he cried out, "Oh, Laura, I'm sorry! I think I handed you the baby upside down!"

And then mama's shocked look, and then her smile when she found baby was right after all, made everybody laugh. The uncles hurried off to their business as the carriage drove away. Grandma went up to her room, closed the door, and prayed for a safe trip home.

The cat came softly into the empty living room, and Aunt Sammy took her in her arms and hid her face in her fur.

Chapter 7

THE NEXT TIME little Lou went to Grandma's was when Aunt Sammy was getting married. He was a year older now, and his head was covered with short curls, his cheeks were red as roses, and he could run around everywhere and even take long walks with his papa and mama.

The night he arrived he was so sleepy that he didn't care about anything except getting to bed. He shut his eyes and kept saying, "bed! bed!" So his mama undressed him and put him in his crib. Then she came down into the living room and they all had a long talk. It would be hard to tell what they *didn't* talk about, and whether it was mostly about the wedding and who was invited, and what Aunt Sammy was going to wear, or Lou's little sayings and doings, and what *he* would wear at the wedding, and how he was likely to behave.

His papa said he was afraid he would talk too much and be troublesome, and his mama said it would excite him to stay up so late in the evening, and that he would be better off in bed. But nobody would listen to a word they said. Everybody insisted that they let all the wedding guests see this beautiful little boy. They were sure he would behave well and not talk at all. As for his being up late just one night, what would that matter?

The next morning Lou awoke very early as he always did, and crept into his mama's bed. He chattered and frolicked until she was so far awake that she thought she might as well get up. She took him in her arms and went into Aunt Sammy's room to show him to her.

Aunt Sammy was asleep, but she woke up and held out her arms to the little fellow. But Lou pulled back and hid his face on his mama's shoulder. "Lou shouldn't be afraid of his Aunt Sammy," said Mama. "That's his dear Aunt Sammy." Lou raised his head and looked mischievously at his aunty, who still held out her arms, longing to catch the little darling and cover him with hugs and kisses.

"Aunty 'ammy, no! Aunty 'ammy, no!" said Lou.

"How funny it is to hear him talk," said Aunt Sammy. "Oh, what lovely hair! Laura, I can't believe you have a child with curly hair! Lou, you little love, look what aunty has under her pillow." And she pulled out her watch and held it up in front of him. Lou smiled, but he was too old to be tricked with watches.

"Does he like to look at pictures? I have lots of pictures to show him. Just wait until I'm dressed." And Aunt Sammy jumped out of bed and rushed around, and was washed and dressed in a twinkling. Lou looked on with great surprise. He had never seen any lady dress except his mama, and thought the clothes of all others grew on them, since they were always there when he saw them. He was so interested that he didn't notice that his mama had seated him on the bed and slipped away to her own room. When he missed her, he began to cry.

"What does Lou want? Does he want his mama?" asked Aunt Sammy.

"Wam," said Lou.

"*Wam?*" repeated Aunt Sammy. "What can that be, I wonder? What is wam?" she asked. But Lou continued to cry and rub his eyes with both of his little fists. "Does Lou want to see some pretty pictures? See, Aunty will show him lots of pictures." But Lou kept his fists close to his eyes and kept crying. "Oh no, what should I do?" thought Aunt Sammy. "I can't take him to his mama unless his papa is up, and who knows if he is in the middle of dressing. Does Lou know where Papa is?"

"Wam," said Lou.

"What *is* wam, I wonder? Is it cake Lou wants?"

"Wam."

"I have no idea what he's saying! I'll carry him in to Mother. Look, Mother. Laura brought Lou in to me, and he keeps crying for wam, and I don't know what wam is. What should I do?"

"His old Grandma will soon comfort him. Come here, blessed little darling. Come to your own Grandma."

But Lou pulled back and held on tightly to Aunt Sammy. Yet he stopped crying, and stared hard at Grandma.

"Isn't he beautiful?" asked Aunt Sammy. "And isn't his hair just as cute as it can be? Did any of us have hair like this? Oh yes, I remember little Charlie did."

"Yes," said Grandma in a tender voice, while tears filled her eyes. "My little Charlie's hair lay on his head like rings of gold."

"*He's been dead twenty-five years, and Mother still sheds tears for him!*" thought Aunt Sammy, and she sighed and held little Lou closer, for fear that they might lose him too.

Chapter 8

Lou's mama now came in smiling. "Oh Laura," said Aunt Sammy, "poor Lou has been crying for some 'wam.' What is it, for pity's sake?"

"Wam," repeated his mama, looking puzzled. "I have no idea. What was it Lou wanted?" she said to Lou.

"Lou want mama. Aunty 'ammy said, 'Lou want Mama?' Lou said 'wam!'"

"Oh, I see now!" said his mama. "He always says 'wam' for yes."

"How funny!" cried Aunt Sammy. "What a funny little guy he is! Hurry and get him dressed, Laura. The boys are all dying to see him. They'll have so much fun with him!"

"Yes, I know they will. I have no doubt that among you all he will be quite spoiled. We have tried very hard with him but he is often very disobedient and self-willed." Grandma and Aunty didn't believe a word of this. When Lou visited a year ago, he behaved like a little angel. Why wouldn't he now? Soon, however, they heard fearful shrieks coming from Mama's room.

"What can Laura be doing to Lou?" cried Aunt Sammy. "I'm going to see. How can she let him scream like that?" She ran through the hall and gave a loud, angry knock at her sister's door. "I really believe you're doing something terrible to that child," she cried.

"Come in and see for yourself," was the answer. Aunt Sammy rushed in. Scattered all over the floor were the fragments of Grandma's best pitcher. The carpet was soaked with water, a chair lay overturned, and Lou, without any clothing, stood screaming in the middle of it all.

"See what I mean?" said his mama.

"Yes, I see," said Aunt Sammy.

"I only wish *you* had to wash and dress him," said his mama.

"Lou don't want to be washed!" shouted Lou.

Aunt Sammy looked very serious. "Did he break the pitcher?" she asked.

"Yes, and would have broken the bowl too, if I had not caught it in time."

"Mother has had that pitcher since she first got married," said Aunt Sammy, picking up the fragments. "Well, there's nothing we can do about it now. I never would have believed that beautiful little body could hold such a temper. But he'll outgrow it. How soft his skin is! How about if I help you bathe and dress him?"

"I wish you would. When that's over, he'll be good and pleasant all day, most likely." Between the two of them, Lou's little clothes were somehow put on him, and when they went down to breakfast he was the picture of health and beauty and sweetness. His uncles did nothing but laugh at everything he said and did. He couldn't eat a bite without it being followed by cheers from them.

"Look at him picking up his potato with his fingers and putting it into his spoon," said one.

"And he holds his spoon as if it were a drumstick," said another.

Then when Aunt Sammy told about his visit to her in her bedroom, and all about him saying wam, there was such an uproar of laughter that Grandma said she was ashamed of them all, and wondered what Lou's papa must think.

After breakfast, Mama took him upstairs with her. While she opened her trunks, she talked with Aunt Sammy about what they would wear at the wedding.

"I didn't buy myself a new dress," she said. "I thought you wouldn't mind. My green silk one is just as good as new. I go out so little since Lou came, and with a fancy collar and this pretty lace cap, I think I'll look fine. As for Lou, I guess you will want him to be dressed in white."

"Oh yes, white of course. Not that he doesn't look very cute in his blue dresses. He looks like a little cherub, whatever he wears."

"I have no idea how he'll behave at the wedding, though. Sammy, I do wish that you and the boys wouldn't laugh at everything he says and does."

"We can't help it. Everything he says and everything he does is so funny. We aren't used to children. It's been so long since we had one in the house. And all his little ways are so different from the ways of adults. There's no use worrying, Laura. The first grandchild is always spoiled."

"Lou, where did you get that enormous piece of cake?" cried his mother, turning suddenly around.

Lou instantly put both hands behind him, holding the cake out of sight.

"Mother gave it to him," said Aunt Sammy.

"Just as he had finished a hearty breakfast! It is too bad! I never let him eat between meals, never. When we were children, mother never gave us cake like this."

"Oh, it won't kill him to have cake this one time," said Aunt Sammy. "I don't think we'll have time to spoil Lou unless you let William go home without you, and stay and visit after he has gone."

"I can't do that. Nothing less than a wedding would have brought us here at all. Won't Lou give Mama some of his cake?"

Yes, Lou would. He broke off a crumb about large enough to feed a bird and put it into her mouth. After lots of coaxing, he gave Aunt Sammy a piece also, and so, little by little, they got a quite a bit of it away from him.

Chapter 9

AT LAST IT WAS time for Lou's nap. "It's very hard to get him to sleep," said his mama. "I have to tell him stories or sing to him to get him quiet."

"Oh, I can get him to sleep," said Aunt Sammy. "If it's nothing but telling stories and singing, you may safely leave that to me. Go down and sit with mother." Mama smiled.

"Come here, Lou," she said. "Mama is going to take off your shoes and put your little tired feet to bed."

"Lou's itty feet no tired," said Lou, and he ran off and hid behind a trunk. When his mama tried to catch him, he ran and climbed onto a chair, planning to climb up on top of the dresser. Mama caught him while Aunt Sammy stood and laughed to see such a race.

"Now I've caught you!" said Mama, and she kissed him and began to tell him a little story while she untied his shoes.

"Give him to me, I can tell stories," said Aunt Sammy. And somehow, she got him into her arms and began her story.

Lou's face began to light up, and his cheeks grew rosier. He sat up very stiff and straight and looked at Aunt Sammy as if he would look right through her.

"Oh, you'll never get him to sleep at this rate," said his mama. "Your story is too interesting, and wakes him up. Just whisper something about horses and whips, something without much sense to it."

"Well, you go down and see Mother and I will. Hearing you talk makes him turn his head around. That's what keeps him awake."

"*I'll let Laura see that I can get Lou to sleep in five minutes,*" she thought. "*I'll just hum a little nonsense, and walk up and down the room a couple times.*" So she took the heavy little boy in her arms and began to sing the first thing that came into her head,

"There is a big white horse,
As big as ten together;
He trots all day, he trots all night,
And never minds the weather.

And there's a golden coach,
For the horse to draw about;
Ten little girls can sit inside,
And ten little boys sit out.

And there's a great long whip,
For the driver tall and black;
With it he never strikes the horse,
But only makes it crack."

Lou liked very much to lie in his auntie's arms and be carried around the room. He didn't know how it tired her or how she was getting out of breath. He lay so still that she said to herself, as she sang the last verse, "*He's almost asleep. I can lay him down in a minute.*"

But Lou burst out in an eager voice with, "And Lou will be the driver!" Aunt Sammy looked at him. Lou was wide-awake! She began to sing again, and once more at the close of the last verse, Lou cried out, "And Lou will be the driver!"

"Yes, yes, Lou will be the driver. But go to sleep now, sweetheart." And once more she began to sing. But it was not working at all. The more she sang the wider Lou's bright eyes opened, and the eager shout kept coming, "And Lou'll drive!"

"I may as well give up," said Aunt Sammy at last, sinking into a chair. "If I had sung that to a girl baby, she would have gone to sleep in a minute. What should I *do*? Laura will never trust me with him again!"

After a while, Mama came upstairs and found the two of them sitting on the carpet, making houses of blocks. "Aha!" she said, "I knew you couldn't get Lou to sleep!"

Chapter 10

When the four uncles came home to dinner and heard how excited Lou had been by hearing Aunt Sammy's song of the horse, they all began to make up stories to amuse him. Uncle Robert told him about bears, and about a fox without a tail, and about a boy that fell into the water and was pulled out by a dog. And he pretended he was very sick, and made Lou put little pills made of paper into his mouth. Then Lou would pretend he was sick too, and Uncle Robert would give him pills. And sometimes Lou would climb up on the sofa, which he called the "poka," and say it was a wagon, and Uncle Robert would stand in front of it and let himself be the horse. Uncle Tom made him a real wagon and would pull him around in it an hour at a time, while Lou held the reins and a little whip in his hands and kept calling out, "Giddy up, old horse!"

When Uncle Fred saw how the little boy enjoyed that, he made a harness for his big dog Bruce, and taught him to pull Lou up and down on the sidewalk in front of the house. Bruce was a very smart dog. He would run and bring his master's slippers when ordered and could carry home a basket of eggs or any package. If a penny was given to him, he would go to a shop with it, where two little cakes were sold to him for it! One day the owner of the shop gave him only one cake, just to

see what he would do. Bruce was not happy. He laid it back on the counter, took his penny and trotted away, and that was the last they ever saw of him at that shop.

When Lou was tired of riding and playing horse, Uncle Frank had even more stories to tell than Uncle Robert, and the little boy never got tired of stories. He would have liked to lie awake all night to listen to them.

At last the day for Aunt Sammy's wedding came. Everybody was dressed nicely, and Lou's mama put on his best outfit and shoes, and curled his hair around her fingers. They all thought he looked good enough to eat, except people never eat little boys. But there was so much going on that day that he didn't get any nap, and staying up way past his usual bedtime made him quite wild. He would go first from his papa to his mama, and from his mama to Uncle Robert, and from Uncle Robert to somebody else. While the minister was speaking serious words, that little tongue ran as fast as it could, and that was very fast indeed.

It wasn't his fault because he didn't know any better, and it wasn't his papa's fault, or his mama's. They never thought it was a good idea for Lou to stay up for the wedding. But it all turned out all right. Aunt Sammy got married just the same, and Lou now had a new uncle, as everybody kept telling him. He also had a little bit of the frosting off the wedding cake, which was the best part of it to him.

The next day the new uncle took Aunt Sammy away to live with him in his own home. Lou and his papa and mama went back to theirs, because it was time to start work on their garden, and lots of other things.

Chapter 11

WHEN LOU WAS two years old, he had stopped saying 'wam' for yes, and he could say most words. But he still said "*h*" when other people said "*s*." His mama thought he was now old enough to be taught something about God, and about heaven, and about the holy angels.

"My darling Lou," she said, taking him in her arms, "do you know who made you?"

Lou was very surprised at this question. But after a moment he said, "Mama made little Lou."

"No, it was God that made you."

"God!" repeated Lou. He always repeated every new word he heard.

"Yes, God made Lou, and sent him to Papa and Mama when he was a little baby."

"This big?" asked Lou, showing the tip of one of his fingers.

"No, bigger than that, but still very small. I love God very much, because He is good. And I love Him for sending me my dear little boy."

"I love Him, too," said Lou. He looked pleased and interested, and said, "Tell more, Mama."

"Do you know what we do every morning when we all kneel down together?"

"Papa talks."

"Yes, Papa talks to God. He thanks Him for taking care of us all night, and for giving us our breakfast, and for lots of other things. And then he asks God to help us all to be good because God loves us to be good."

"Does he love me?"

"Yes, He loves you very much."

"If Papa talks to God, I want to talk to God."

Then his mama made him kneel beside her, and she folded his little hands together and taught him to say, "Please, Oh God, take care of Lou, and make him a good boy."

After this she said no more, but held him quietly in her arms, rocking him back and forth. After a while, he began to laugh, and exclaimed, "God call to Lou. God hay, 'Lou, come up in the moon'. God hay ho" (says so).

"Does Lou think God ever made any other little boys?"

"Lou don't know."

"Yes, God made all the little boys and all the little girls in the world. God made everything."

"He made Lou's kitty," he said. "And he made birds. And God made God." Then turning to look in his mama's face, he said, "Yes, God made helf" (himself).

"There is another thing Mama wants to tell Lou. God can see everything her little boy does. When Lou goes out in the orchard and picks up the green apples that lie under the trees and eats them, God always sees him."

"Lou never saw God looking."

"No, but He can see you. You know Mama has told you never to eat green apples because they'll make you sick, and yet you often do it. And God knows when you disobey Mama. And He does not love to see you do that."

By this time Lou was tired of the talk. He jumped down from his mama's lap and looked about to see what mischief he could do. His favorite trick was throwing things out the window, and he now grabbed his papa's boots and threw them out, one after another. His papa, who was at work in the garden, was much surprised to see them come flying out.

"That was naughty," said Mama. "Go stand in the corner." Lou went, but he cried the whole time he was there.

Chapter 12

THE SUMMER DAYS at this time were long and lovely. Lou could follow his papa around the garden and watch him as he weeded the flowerbeds or raked the walks. He helped both Papa and Mama by holding the hammer and the nails, when they trained vines to grow around the door. Sometimes he filled his little wheelbarrow with apples and worked until his face was quite red. He carried them to the old pig that lived out in the yard near the stable and never seemed to do anything but eat and grunt.

His mama sometimes watched him from her window, and sometimes ran out to see where he was or what he was doing. This took almost all her time and she couldn't spend her whole time watching him. She had to clean her house and plan what she would have for breakfast and lunch and supper. She had to make a lot of little clothes for Lou, since now that he played outdoors all day long, he got his clothes dirty and had to have them changed very often. Long ago when Lou lived, most people made all their own clothes and it took them quite a lot of time for each little shirt.

Lou's mama also wanted time to read and write, and play her piano. She also had a cabinet of shells that she liked arranging, not to mention the rare plants she was collecting. So she thought it would be a good idea to get some young girl who was older than Lou, but not too old to play with him, to come and run about the garden and the yard with him, and see that he didn't go near the well or anywhere else where he could get hurt.

She soon heard of a poor woman whose husband had died, and who was like the old woman that lived in the shoe, and had so many children she didn't know what to do. She was very thankful to let one of them go to stay with such a nice kind lady as Mrs. James, Lou's mama.

"I'll send you my Becky. She's seven and a half years old, ma'am."

"I'm afraid she's too young," said Lou's mama.

"Is it too young she is! But she's growing older every day she lives, ma'am."

"I wanted a little girl who liked to run and play, but yet was old enough to keep my little boy out of mischief. He's very mischievous, and I doubt if he would obey a child so young."

"She's like a real little woman she is, active, lively, sprightly, with a mind of her own, and has had the care of all the kids whenever I've been off to a day's work, ma'am. And a full meal has never entered her poor little stomach since the day her father fell off the roof, and I almost fainted when I saw the sight of him; I did indeed."

Becky looked up at Mrs. James while her mother was speaking, with longing eyes. To run about that pretty garden with that cute little boy, to get plenty to eat and have nice clothes to wear! It all seemed so wonderful! Mrs. James saw the look and her heart melted.

"I will give her a week's trial," she said.

"Thank you so much ma'am," cried Mrs. Medill. "I'll scrub her up clean and tidy, so she won't know herself if she meets herself on the street."

That afternoon, her face shining from a good wash and her calico dress and apron as tidy as tidy could be, Becky Medill arrived at her new home, and in half an hour she and Lou were good friends. Mrs. James sat down at a table and began to draw a picture.

"How nice it is," she thought, "that I've found that little girl! Her mother will have one less child to feed and clothe, and I will be able to do a lot for the child. I will teach her to read and spell, and as fast as Lou outgrows his clothes, I can send them to Mrs. Medill."

Chapter 13

Her pleasant thoughts were interrupted by Lou, who came running in very angry. "I don't like that girl!" he shouted. "She won't come when I call her!"

"Oh, don't talk like that!" said his mama.

"He kept calling me '*chick! chick! chick!*' and I'm not a chicken!" Becky burst out. His mama laughed.

"Becky," she said, "don't you see that Lou is only a very little boy, only two years old, and that he's just pretending calling you a chicken? Now go back out and play, both of you. And Becky, remember what I said about the well." Becky went out slowly, and consoled herself with eating green apples in the orchard.

"Mama says don't eat green apples," said Lou. "God can see you if you disobey me."

"You're only a little boy," said Becky, "You're only two years old. Your mama said so."

Once more Lou rushed to his mama. "God is looking right at her!" he cried, in a loud eager voice. "He sees her eating apples. He does!"

"Tell her that Mama says not to eat green apples. They will make her sick." Lou ran off with this message and Becky stopped eating, and filled her pockets instead.

When it was time for supper, they were called in. Becky had hers in the kitchen with the cook, and ate as if it was her last chance on earth, while the cook looked at her angrily. "At this rate I'll need two pairs of hands, and we'll have to buy a barrel of flour a month. If that child has eaten one slice of bread, she's eaten five. Mercy! If she isn't helping herself to another! Where's your manners, child?"

"My what?" asked Becky.

"Your *manners*, I say. To come into a gentleman's house and eat as if you were a tiger—a raving, roaring, raging tiger!"

Maybe you've always had enough to eat," said Becky, coolly. "Maybe your mother wasn't a poor widow. Maybe your father didn't fall off a house and get killed. Maybe you wasn't never a little girl like me."

"That's for sure!" cried Abigail, pouring out a cup of milk for the child. "But if your mother's a widow and your father has died, I guess that's why you are like that!

"Are Mr. and Mrs. James neat and tidy people?" asked Becky.

"Neat and tidy! Neat and tidy? How dare you ask such a question?" cried Abigail. "Of course they are, you little urchin, you!"

"I only wanted to know because if they are, I thought I'd borrow their brush and comb," said Becky.

Abigail tried to say something, but the words wouldn't come. She was just so amazed that Becky didn't have anything to comb her hair with. She told Mrs. James, who hurried out the moment lunch was over to buy Becky a brush, a comb, and several other things that she might be tempted to "borrow." Her heart sank within her when she saw that by taking in Becky, she had really taken another child to teach.

"I hope, Abigail," she said, "that you will be patient with the poor girl and try to teach her some of your own nice ways. It will be a great help to Mrs. Medill if we can train this child to be a useful young woman."

"If you're not too tired to stay up for prayers, Becky, you don't need to go to bed," said Mrs. James, when Lou was laid down in his crib to talk himself to sleep. Becky didn't know what "staying up for prayers" meant, but she was curious to find out and was quite ready to stay up. She never went to bed early at home and didn't feel sleepy at all. She went out and sat on the doorstep that led to the yard, and waited there until Abigail called her in.

Professor James read a short chapter from the Bible, and then Becky, watching every word and look, saw them all kneel down with closed eyes. She did as the rest did, and when she went up to bed with Abigail she said, "It's a fine thing to have your prayers said off for you when you're tired and sleepy. It is a lot better than my mother's way. She often goes to sleep saying hers."

"We've just had family worship, but we still need to say our own prayers now," said Abigail.

Becky was almost asleep and very confused, but seeing Abigail kneel down on her side of the bed, she knelt down at hers, where she soon forgot all her joys and all her troubles in a sound sleep. After a while she was shaken by Abigail until she was awake, and couldn't remember whether she had said her prayers or not. Poor little Becky!

Chapter 14

THE NEXT MORNING Becky awoke early, feeling strong and well. She remembered what a good supper she had the night before, and wondered if she would have as good a breakfast. She dressed quickly, and ran down to the kitchen.

"Here you are!" said Abigail. "Well, take up this water for Lou's bath, and don't you spill one drop on the stairs. Here's what you're going to do. You can dress that child just as well as his mama can, and don't you let her be breaking her back doing it, while you stand staring at her."

"I was supposed to run and play with him and that's all," replied Becky.

"Is that so! Well then, stay here and get the breakfast, since now that there's two mouths to fill, there should be four hands to work. I'll just run up and dress the child myself."

On hearing this, Becky scampered out of the kitchen as fast as she could. She knew she couldn't prepare breakfast, and she knew she could dress one child, since at home she had five to dress. Mrs. James, who thought she came all on her own, was very pleased to hear her say that she had come for Lou.

"What a little treasure she will be!" she thought. "Of course I'll bathe Lou myself, but if she says she can dress him, I'll let her try." But Lou didn't like this plan at all, and he told Becky to "Get out!"

"Lou, never let me hear you speak to Becky like that again," said his mama.

"I didn't say it to Becky. I said 'Get out' to an old bear," said Lou. His mama stood looking at him, puzzled to know what to say or do. Lou saw from her serious, anxious face that he had made her sad. This made him quiet while Becky dressed him with her grownup ways.

"I see you're used to dressing children," said Mama.

"Yes ma'am," said Becky.

Lou looked fresh and bright when his little white apron was tied, and his hair fell in ringlets all over his neck. Then he came and knelt down at her knee to say his prayers.

"Lou," she said, laying her hand on his head, "you *know* there was no old bear here when you said 'Get out!' You said that to Becky. It was very naughty to pretend you said it to a bear. Now, when you pray to God, ask Him to forgive you for doing that."

Lou looked very serious. He knelt down and folded his hands and shut his eyes and said, "O God, please to forgive me for saying 'Get out' to Becky."

"And for saying afterwards that you were speaking to a bear," said his mama.

"And please to forgive me for saying, 'Get out you old bear.'"

"No, not that. You don't understand," said his mama. "O Lou! What *shall* I do to make you understand?"

Becky, worried at seeing Mrs. James looking so anxious, cried out, "Maybe a good hard slap would do, Ma'am."

"Of course I'm not going to slap him," said Mrs. James. She told Becky to take Lou down and play with him near the house until breakfast time. Then she went to the study where Lou's papa was reading, and told him all about it. He only laughed and said there was no need to be so worried. Lou didn't seem much more than a baby to him, and he thought to himself, "*Such a young baby doesn't know enough to tell a lie.*"

But Lou's mama felt sorrowful all day. She was afraid Lou was not going to grow up to be a good, truthful boy.

Chapter 15

As the summer passed away and cold weather began to come on, there were sometimes whole days when Lou couldn't go outside at all. Then Becky helped him build houses and castles with blocks, and she liked to do that as much as he did, and would often argue with him about who had the most blocks, or who could build the highest houses. Then Mama had to intervene. She would say, "Becky, you forget what a little boy Lou is. You're six years older than he is, and ought to behave better than he does."

"Yes, ma'am, I am eight years old, going on nine."

One day Lou played very hard, gathering the dry leaves that had fallen from the trees, and rolling them away in his wheelbarrow, and got very tired. The next day he felt rather grumpy, and since it was very cold and the wind was blowing very hard, his mama kept him inside. He wouldn't amuse himself at all that day, and begged her to tell him stories and sing to him, until she was quite tired. Whenever she tried to go away, he held on to her dress, so that she couldn't move.

"Let go of my dress, Lou," she said at last. "I'm tired, and I'm going out to walk now."

"I don't hear Mama," he said.

"I said you must let go of my dress."

"I don't hear Mama," he repeated. His mama stooped down and unclasped his hands from her dress.

"Now you're naughty again, just as you were the day you said 'Get out!' to Becky. God hears my little Lou when he talks like that, and God is not pleased." Lou burst out crying. He wanted to be naughty and he wanted to please God too.

A few days later, Lou took a book and pretended to read. He said, "Once there was a boy named Johnny; a very good little boy. When his mama told him to let go of her dress, he let go. He didn't say, 'Johnny don't hear Mama.'"

When his mama heard that, the tears came into her eyes. She said to herself, "*It's true Lou is only a little more than two years old, but if he knows enough to say that, he must know when he doesn't speak the truth.*"

Lou saw her tears, and ran to her and said, in a soft, sweet voice," *Don't* feel bad, Mama."

She replied, "Mama is worried about her little Lou. She wants so much to have him love God, and be a good boy."

"Lou *do* love God; Mama won't feel bad any more. Lou loves Mama and loves God too."

Then he knelt down and said his little prayer, and added, "Bless Kitty, too." The rest of that day he was sweet and gentle, and so good and so affectionate that everybody in the house was glad that such a boy lived there. His papa was very happy, when it came night, to play with the little fellow, and tell him stories about what he used to do when he was a young boy himself and lived on a farm, and hunted woodchucks. And the last thing before he went to sleep that night, as he did every night, he prayed to God to bless his precious child, and to help him to grow up into a good man.

Chapter 16

At last, the summer that had Lou's second birthday in it was really gone, and instead of green grass and flowers, nothing could be seen but a blanket of white snow that was spread smoothly over everything. People put on their warmest coats and cloaks, and got out their sleighs, and you could hear the merry jingling of bells, and the laughter of the boys as they coasted down the hills or skated over the ponds.

Lou stood at the window and looked out. Oh, how he longed to be a big boy, and to have a pair of skates, and to be a big man, with a horse and a sleigh of his own! His papa often took him out on sleigh rides with his mama, when he was bundled up quite warm, and could hold the reins, and imagine he was the driver. At these times he talked nonstop. He asked questions about everything he saw on the road, and kept his papa and mama laughing at all his smart little sayings.

His papa made a little sled for him with his own hands, and Lou could load it with wood, and pull it over the snow to the front door. Then he would march in stamping his feet and say to his mama, "Do you want a nice load of wood today, ma'am?"

And she would say, "How much is it, sir?"

"Oh, about two dollars."

"All right, I'll take it. You may deliver it to the kitchen door."

And then she would pay him two dollars, which sometimes meant two kisses, sometimes two apples, and most of the time two little bits of paper, cut in circles like money.

Becky had gone home. Finding it impossible get along without all of her help, her mother had come and taken her away. Lou was happier and behaved better without her, because he had no one to take his toys when he wanted them, or to argue with him. At last his papa's winter vacation came, and he took mama and Lou to see *his* mother this time. There were no aunts and uncles there, but this grandma, Grandma James, loved him just as much as the other grandma did.

Up in her attic there were so many baskets of nuts from her trees, and hordes of red squirrels scampered about up there, stealing the nuts and having a good time. They thought all these nuts were stored away there just for them, and that made them happy and noisy. Then, down in Grandma James's cellar, how many apples there were from her trees, and what good apples they were! Papa now had plenty of time to play with Lou, and to take him all over the farm. Carried about in his kind papa's arms, Lou saw the pigs and the hens and the horses every day. When they were both tired of that, they would go in and sit by the fire, and Papa would tell over and over again what he used to do when he was a boy, while Grandma listened until her bright eyes shone like two stars.

When they went home, they took a lot of the nuts and apples and other good things. Lou had always said that when he was a big man he wanted to be a stagecoach driver, but now he said he would be a farmer, and raise hens and chickens and cows and pigs, and have apples and nuts like Grandma James.

Chapter 17

But the wintry days passed away. The snow in the valley and on the mountains melted and turned into water, and ran off, making a joyful noise as it went, like a boy let out of school. The green grass sprang up and the trees were covered with tender little buds. Once more Lou could run about in the orchard and in the garden, and watch his papa and mama as they worked among their flowers with the hoe and trowel and spade. They cleaned out old plants and sowed and planted new ones. His cousin Jacob often came to see him now, and they played together like two playful dogs.

"Who has been to see you this afternoon?" his papa asked him one night as they sat at the table.

"Jacob."

"What did you do all that time?"

"We played."

"What did you play?"

Lou sat up very straight in his chair, and answered in a loud voice, growing more and more eager at every word, "Oh, we played, he in one corner, and I in another corner, and go see each other. And he came to see me, and I shaked hands with him; and I went to see him, and he shaked hands with me, and knocked at the door, and had supper. And then we played run, run, run! Jacob and I ran together and laughed and then played have garden."

His papa said, "I'm glad you and Jacob had such a good time together. Some little boys are lame, and can't run around, and some are blind and can't see. What would you do, if you were blind?"

"I would pray to God to give me eyes."

After tea, his mama sat mending something, and had a basket of little bundles near her. Lou picked one up.

"This is my baby," he said. "Her name is Mellie. Let me untie it, and see if she has a naughty heart inside of her."

He untied the bundle, and took out a little bit of flannel.

"This is her naughty heart," he said. "I've taken it out, and now she will be good."

And then, "Oh Mama! Jacob don't know who made him!"

"But you know."

"Yes, God made Jacob, but I never see Him looking down."

Then he placed all the chairs in the room in a long row, and climbed up, and ran back and forth on them.

"Don't do that, Lou. I'm afraid you'll fall."

"I can't get down. I won't fall. I am a loco, running on a railroad."

"A what?"

"A loco."

"A locomotive, you mean."

Lou was embarrassed that he had made such a mistake, and even angry. He jumped down, put the chairs back in their places, and went and sat down on a stool in a corner.

"Lou," said his mama, "I made a worse mistake than that when I was a little girl. I took some candy and a needle book in my bag to church." (You probably don't know what a needle book was, but Lou knew. His mama used it to hold her sewing needles all in one place, like a little book.)

Lou jumped up and came to his mama, curious to know what she did with it. "What made you take a needle book to church? Seems to me that was a funny thing to take."

"I took it because it had just been given to me, and I couldn't bear to leave it home. I took the candy so that if I were sleepy in church I could eat one now and then, and get woken up. Well, I was listening to the sermon very hard, but I felt my eyes beginning to wink—and wink—and w-i-n-k—and I knew I would fall asleep, and not hear the rest of the sermon. So I put my hand into my bag to take out a candy, but I didn't look at the bag, I looked at the minister and listened as hard as I could. So I put my needle book into my mouth, and thought it was a candy!" Lou laughed so hard that it made his mama laugh just to see him. His papa, hearing how merry they were, laughed too, though he had not heard a word of the story.

Part 2

Chapter 1

It was a bright May morning. Lou awoke, feeling well and happy. His mama kissed him and said, "How are you doing this morning, my sweet little lamb?"

"I am very well, you sweet mama," said Lou, and he threw his arms around her neck and kissed her many times. Then he stopped, as if he wanted to ask something, but couldn't think of the right words. "What—what are you, if I'm a little lamb?"

"The lamb's mother is called a sheep," Mama answered.

Lou kissed her again, and said "I love you very much, you sweet sheep." The "sweet sheep" went down to breakfast with her lamb, and for a while he was playful and good. But when he asked for something on the table that he couldn't have, he became very angry and threw himself back in his chair and began to pout. All the pink cheeks and bright eyes and curly hair in the world will not make a child beautiful when he is in a bad mood. Lou was not a nice sight to look at, as he sat there scowling and frowning.

"I never saw little lambs act like that," said his mama. "They eat the green grass as their mothers tell them to do, and never ask for anything else."

"I'll eat grass, too," said Lou, turning nice again.

"No, eat your oatmeal and milk. Oatmeal and milk to a little boy is just what grass is to a little lamb." After breakfast Lou played about, frisking here and there pretending he was a lamb. He crawled on all fours, and then put his mouth down into his mama's workbasket saying, "I wonder if there is anything good for lambs to eat in this basket? Yes, here is a strawberry. I'll eat that." It was not a real strawberry. It was only a homemade strawberry, made of red flannel, with dots of yellow thread all over it to look like seeds.

"Don't put that in your mouth; you'll ruin it," said Mama. But Lou scampered away with it and got it very wet. "Lou, come back right now, and bring me the strawberry." Lou shook his head. He couldn't talk because his mouth was full. "I won't call you a lamb anymore," said Mama. Then Lou dropped the strawberry and began to cry.

"I *will* be good, if you'll call me a lamb," he cried. He looked so ridiculous, down on the floor on all fours like an animal, yet crying and talking like a real child, that his mama couldn't help laughing.

"I never heard a lamb talk or saw one cry before," she said.

Then Lou stopped crying, and began to laugh. "No," he said, "I'm not a common lamb."

Chapter 2

Now that the weather was getting warm, Lou's long curls bothered him, and he often asked his mama to cut

them off, but she couldn't make up her mind to do it. She liked to watch him from her window, with his bright hair flying in the wind, and she said if she ever cut his hair off he would look like a big boy and not her little Lou.

His papa said he would grow into a big boy, hair or no hair, and he thought he looked like a girl now. Then mama decided to cut off the curls, and one morning before breakfast, she took her scissors and clipped them off, one by one. Lou was thrilled, partly because he liked everything new, partly because he felt more comfortable to have that hot hair off of his neck. He expected to surprise his papa, with the sight of his little, cropped head. But Papa ate his breakfast without saying a word until at last Lou burst out, "Papa, why don't you be surprised to see my haircut?"

Then Papa looked at the little guy and laughed, and said he was very surprised. "Papa, I'm a big boy now, like other boys. I'm almost three years old. I'm almost old enough to wear pants. Jacob wears pants."

"You call yourself a big boy, but you behave like a little boy," said his papa. "You cry when you're hurt, just like you did when you were a baby, and didn't know how to talk. It's normal for babies to cry when they are hurt or hungry or in pain. They can't talk, and so they have to cry. But you can say anything you want, so you ought to stop crying. I'm going to the Post Office now; do you want to go with me?"

"Oh yes, Papa!" As they walked along together, Lou asked, "Where does the man at the Post Office get all his letters? Does he make them himself?"

"No. Different people write them, and send them to him, and he looks on the outside of each letter to see whose name is on it, and then he gives it to the man or woman to whom it is written."

"Does he give them all to big men and women? Won't he give any to little boys?"

"If a letter comes for a little boy, he gives it to the little boy. Here we are! Now let us see what there is for us."

There were a lot of letters for Lou's papa, and several for Mama, and there were some papers too. And last of all, best of all, there was one very little letter to

> *Master Louis James,*
> *Care of Professor James*
> *Wilton, Mass.*

"Hey, here is a letter for you, Lou!" said his papa.

The truth is, the letter had come the day before, and Papa had left it at the Post Office so that Lou could have the fun of going to pick it up himself. Lou was delighted. What with having his hair cut, and getting a letter, he felt all grown up!

Chapter 3

When Lou got home with his letter, he was going to put it away in a drawer with some of his best toys. But his mama said, "Oh no, don't put it away until I've read it to you. It's from Aunt Sammy. I knew she would write you a little letter sometime." She opened it and Lou sat on his low chair, and looked intently at her face while she read:

> Dear little Lou,
> I wish I knew just how you are, and how you do!
> I wish your darling little feet were running fast down
>   Auntie's street,
> or climbing softly up the stairs, to take your aunty
>   unawares!
> What a big boy you've grown to be, since I saw you, and you
>   saw me!
> Now Lou, my dear, you must come here.
> I have no toys, or girls, or boys,
> but you can play, all the long day,
> upon the shore, where you've never been before;
> and pick up shells, dig little wells,

*and your mama and your papa,
can swim and splash, and dive and dash
in the ocean blue, and so can you.
So pack your clothes, and follow your nose,
and come right here, you little dear,
as soon as you can, to your Aunty Sam.*

"What is Aunt Sammy's '*shore?*'" asked Lou. "Is it her garden, or her yard? And what is an '*ocean blue?*'"

"Oh you'll see, when we get there," replied his mama. "You will have the nicest time in the world at Aunt Sammy's. We all will."

"Well," said Lou, in a happy voice. "I'll go and get my hat, my kitty, my wheelbarrow and my little hatchet, and then we'll go."

His mama laughed. "We can't start off that easily," she said. "Papa's vacation hasn't started yet, and besides, our trunks aren't ready, and some of your clothes are dirty."

"But I want to go *now*. Let's go *now!*"

"You can't go now, and you must be patient."

"I can't be patient. I want to dig wells and pick up shells. I want to follow my nose"—

"Wherever it goes!" said Mama. "Well, let it go out into the garden, then. And you can run after it and try to catch it."

"Just as kitty chases her tail?" asked Lou, and away he ran. Kitty was out in the garden, stepping softly over the flowerbeds.

"I know something that you don't know, Kitty," said Lou. "Come here and I'll tell you." But Kitty pretended she didn't want to know. "You'd better come, Kitty. It's something really fun." But Kitty wouldn't come. So Lou ran and grabbed her. "You *will* listen, you naughty kitten. We're all going to see our Aunt Sammy. You're going and I'm going. And we're going to see an 'ocean blue,' and lots of other things."

Kitty rubbed her whiskers against his cheek and purred as if to say, "*I'm glad to hear it. I didn't know I had an Aunt Sammy, but if I do, I'd really like to go and see her. But I would like it better if she came here. I like this house the best. I've been all over it and smelled everything in it, and have decided that it is a very nice house. But I don't think I'll like my Aunt Sammy's house as much as this one, or her ocean, even if it* is *blue.*"

Chapter 4

THE NEXT DAY, Lou hoped their journey was going to start, but his mama said again that he must wait patiently. So he went out to the woodhouse to play. There was a lot of wood stacked up high, and a good many woodchips lay scattered about. Lou chopped at them with a new little hatchet his papa had given him, and was busy for a long time. He was surprised when he was called in to lunch. He'd had such a happy morning. His hands and face needed washing before he could go to the table, and so he was a little late. His papa had already asked a blessing and begun to carve the meat.

"Hey, Papa! You haven't said 'in Jesus' name!'" he cried out.

"I said that before you came to the table," said his papa. "What have you been doing all morning?"

I've been hatching, Papa."

"Hatching? Hatching what?"

"Hatching wood, with my new hatchet." His papa laughed, and Lou laughed too, though he didn't know what he was laughing about. After dinner, he was playing in the room and his mama went to the piano, and began to sing "The Mistletoe Bough."

Soon Lou stopped playing so he could listen, and when the song was over, his mama found him crying sadly. She was sorry she had sung a song that made him cry. She thought he was too young to notice the words, which are very sad. She soon dried his tears by singing something funny, in two voices.

> *First voice.*
> What nibbling noise is that I hear?
> What little noise is that?
> *Second voice.*
> Don't you know it when you hear
> The purring of your cat?
> *First voice.*
> I never knew my cat to go
> And hide behind the wall
> Of course I know her purring sounds;
> It is not that, at all.
> *Second voice.*
> To tell the truth it's not the cat,
> It's only little me,
> Trembling within my hiding place,
> As hungry as can be.
> *First voice.*
> And who is 'little me,' I say?
> And who is hungry here?
> Come out, come out, and show yourself;
> There's no one here to fear.
> *Second voice.*
> I cannot come! I dare not come!

You'd drive me right away;
And yet I've not had to eat,
A single scrap today.
No crumbs lie scattered on your floors,
You keep your house so neat;
Your cheese you lock within a box,
With all your dainties sweet.
    First voice.
Ah! Now I know just who you are!
Come out sir, if you please!
You're the mouse that steals my cake,
And eats up all my cheese!
    Second voice.
Oh do not scold me! Do not frown,
Until my story's told!
I never stole a crumb from you,
I'm only nine days old.
My father was a soldier bold,
He perished in the wars—
    First voice.
Aha! You mean he fought with cats,
And perished in their claws.
    Second voice.
My mother hid her little nest
Just here behind the wall,
She nursed us every one herself,
And dearly loved us all.
But she has gone, we know not where,
And left her children here;
And my poor little sisters lie
Half dead with grief and fear.

First voice.
Come out, poor things, and let me see
If all you say is true;
I'm sure that we shall gladly spare
Some of our food for you.
Ah! Here you come, you cute things!
What little beady eyes!
What tiny paws, what funny tails,
How bright you look! How wise!
Here, pick these crumbs of bread, and eat
These little bits of cake!
I think my darling boy has left
His dinner for your sake.
    Chorus of mice.
Thanks, lady, thanks; our dinner nice
We hungry, starving little mice,
Have found and eaten in a trice. (instant)
The bread was good, and so are you;
The cake was sweet, and you are, too.
First voice.
Tomorrow, after dinner then,
You little things may come again,
And now goodbye, until tomorrow!
    Chorus.
Goodbye, dear lady, until tomorrow.

[The six little mice form a ring, and dance away to their hole where they disappear.]

Chapter 5

"I like that," said Lou, when his mama stopped singing. "But I wish I could see the little mice and hear them talk. And I would like to see them dance, too."

"So would I," said his mama, laughing. "And now you may run out into the yard and play until the horse is harnessed."

"Am I going somewhere?"

"Yes, we are going up the mountain, a long way."

"That's nice."

So Lou ran out and played awhile near the door, and then went to the stable to see the horse being harnessed. His papa was there and he said to Lou, "Well, Lou, are you going up the mountain, this afternoon?"

"Yes, Papa. Do you want to hear a story? I know a story about six little mice."

"Yes, I would like to hear it. But not right now. I'm too busy now. Run in and tell Mama to get ready and I'll come in a few minutes." Lou ran in. He found his mama tying a string around a large book. The book was made of newspapers, bound together. On the table near her was a basket. "What is that book for, Mama? Is there anything in the basket?"

"I'm going to collect some ferns and dry them between the pages of the book. Then next winter, when the ground is covered with snow, I'll fill some vases with sand and keep my ferns in the vases."

"I wish I could dry some ferns, too."

"Well, you may. I'll bring another book for you. And the basket is for mosses and such things."

"May I take my little basket and get mosses too?"

"You may take your basket, but I think you would rather pick raspberries than collect mosses."

"Yes, I would. I love raspberries."

He ran to get his basket, and at last they all set off. Lou sat between his papa and mama; he held his basket, and she held hers. Under the seat there was a stone jar with a piece of white linen in it, and another basket, and a large jug. Lou was going to ask what they were all for, but his papa told the old horse to "Giddy up!" and they rolled rapidly out of the yard and down the village street.

"Now, Lou, let's hear your story," said Papa. Lou told the story wonderfully well, and his papa was glad to hear him tell it. By the time it came to an end, they had left the smooth road and were beginning to go slowly, and by a rough path, up the side of the mountain. Papa got out and walked, holding the reins in his hand.

"Papa, can't I hold the reins?" asked Lou.

"Oh no, don't give him the reins!" cried Mama. "I'm scared enough now."

"There's no danger," said Papa. "The road is fairly rough, but this old horse knows every step of the way."

Mama was very glad when it was time to get out, even if the horse did know the way. And Lou was glad to find himself in such a beautiful place. He didn't find many berries, but the berries he did find, he put into his basket, together with one red mushroom and one yellow one, a twig from a dead tree that he thought was shaped a little like a dog, and several other odd things.

They were in a lovely spot. Tall trees grew on each side of the path, and made it cool and shady. Graceful ferns and delicate vines, and all sorts of green leaves filled the spaces beneath the trees, and nothing could be heard but the hum of busy insects and the refreshing sound of a stream that ran cheerfully by.

Mama filled her book with ferns and wished she had another book to fill. Lou gathered whatever leaves he liked and filled his too, making Mama admire every one. Meanwhile, Papa, who could go with his thick boots where they could not, had gone higher up and collected all sorts of mosses and lichens: green and gray and white, and pretty little red flowers. "It's time to go now," he said. "Come, my dear; come, Lou."

"Oh, let's not go yet! It is so quiet and cool here!" said Mama.

"We must go; you know we have to stop on the way."

"I wish college prayers were later!" said Mama. "We always have to hurry off just as the pleasant part of the day comes on. I would like to stay here all night!"

"Wouldn't the old bears catch us?" asked Lou, pushing closer to her side.

"There are no bears here now," said his papa. "If there were, I don't think they would hurt you."

Just outside the village, they stopped at a farmhouse and Papa got the stone jar from beneath the seat. The farmer's wife came out to see what they wanted. Lou stood up and saw that the cows were being milked.

"How are you doing, Mrs. Thompson?" asked Mama. "Can you let us buy a little more of your nice butter? And a few eggs? And if you can spare a little cream, I would be glad to have some."

Mrs. Thompson she said could. She carried the stone jar into the house and brought it back, filled with butter, and covered with the linen cloth. Then she took the basket and the bottle, and filled them with eggs and milk. Lou watched everything with great interest.

"I put a pullet's egg into the basket for you, my little man," said Mrs. Thompson.

"What *is* a pullet's egg? Oh, let me carry it in my hands," cried Lou.

His papa opened the basket and took out a very little egg.

"What a cute little egg!" cried Lou.

"Thank Mrs. Thompson," whispered Mama.

"I did," said Lou.

"If you did, she didn't hear you and neither did I. Say 'Thank you, Mrs. Thompson.'"

Lou was silent.

"Oh, never mind!" said Mrs. Thompson. "All the thanks I want is to see him happy." And then she wished them good evening and went into the house. Lou's papa drove away, and drove on without another word. Mama was serious and silent, too. Lou knew they were both unhappy with him. But he played with his egg and tried to have a good time.

"Oh, you cute little egg! You special little egg!" he kept saying. All at once it broke in his hand, and his face and hands and shirt were covered with it. He felt sticky and uncomfortable and ashamed, and began to cry.

"You see what happens to little boys who disobey," said Mama. "If I had not been upset with you, I would have carried your egg for you and you could have had it for breakfast."

Chapter 6

Whenhe heard this, Lou cried harder than ever, and as they drove through the village, everybody they met heard him. It was time for prayers, and all the students were outside heading to the chapel and they heard him. How embarrassed his papa and mama were!

Does everything pleasant have such an unhappy ending as this trip up the mountain had? Yes it does, sooner or later, unless people choose to be as kind and pleasant when they come home, as they were when they went away. One excuse must be made for Lou. He was very tired, because it was a warm day in the middle of summer. After his papa had helped him and his mama down from the carriage at their house, he went back to the college for prayers. Lou now stopped crying and began to look for his raspberries. He thought they would be nice for his supper, with some of Mrs. Thompson's cream. But the soft fruit was buried under leaves and twigs, and mixed up with bits of mushrooms, moss, and stones. Then Lou burst out crying again, this time not angrily, but in a very sad way that made his mama sorry for him. She led him up to her room and washed the stains of yellow egg from his face and hands, and cooled his forehead with fresh water.

"Next time you'll be a good boy," she said kindly, "and thank Mrs. Thompson when she gives you a tiny little egg. And you won't roll it over your

cheek and crush it again. I'm going to forgive you now, because I'm sorry for you."

"Why don't you punish me before you forgive me, Mama?" Lou asked, in a gentle, pleased voice.

"I'll tell you why. It's because God so often forgives me, without punishing me."

"Mama! Are you ever naughty?" cried Lou. "What do you do?" Before Mama had time to answer, the bell rang for tea. Papa had come in from prayers and was waiting for them downstairs. All the way down, Lou kept kissing his mama's hand. He felt sorry that he had not been a good boy, and he loved his mama so much because she had forgiven him. Don't you sometimes feel like that when you have said or done what you know displeases God? If you do, that shows that you love Him, and are His own dear child.

The next morning at breakfast, neither Lou nor his mama had much appetite. Mama said it was because the night had been so warm. She said Lou didn't lie still for a minute, but tossed and turned all night, and she would be thankful to get him to the seashore.

"By the way, I promised to make him a wooden shovel to dig with," said Papa. "I better not forget my promises. He will enjoy digging in the sand."

"Are we going today, Papa?"

"No, not today."

"Tomorrow, then."

"No."

"The day after that?" His papa shook his head. "We're never going! It's been a year since Aunt Sammy told us to come. What if the ocean blue all dries up before we get there?"

His papa smiled. "We're going on Friday. We'll stop in Boston for a little while. I have business there, and then we will go straight to Aunt Sammy's."

Chapter 7

Lou asked so many times the next day when it would be Friday, and was so restless that his mama got very tired of hearing it. She was trying to get something done that she would need at the seaside, and couldn't read to him as much as usual, and so he had lots of time to get into all sorts of mischief. He took his papa's inkstand, which he had been forbidden to touch, and spilled the ink all over some papers on the study table, and on his own shirt. Then when his shirt had been taken off, and a clean one put on, and his mama was busy trying to save Papa's papers, he ran to her cabinet of shells, pulled out a drawer, and fell backwards with it, scattering the neatly arranged shells all over the floor. How glad she was when Friday came, and this anxious little child could start on the trip with her.

It was a very warm day and the train cars were crowded with people. Lou had a seat by the window, and for a while he was interested in everything. There was so much to see, inside and outside of the train. As they came into the first town, he heard a loud, long whistle that was like a dreadful scream.

"What's that?" he cried, shrinking away from the window.

"It's the locomotive, whistling to let people know it's coming," said his papa.

"I didn't know locomotives had so much sense!" cried Lou. Several people who sat near them smiled at this remark, and he heard someone say, "What a smart little fellow that is! He talks as clearly as a grown man."

"Yes," said another, "I love the funny mistakes of little children! Last winter one of my children asked another if birds of prey were good to eat, and was told they were not. 'Why, yes they are, we had some for dinner the other day. We had preying (prairie) hens!" Both gentlemen laughed, and so did Lou, though he didn't know why. The dust and ashes began to fly in through the windows and settle on his moist cheeks and on his clothes, and got in his eyes. He was tired and thirsty, and looking out the window wasn't fun anymore.

He yawned, and said "Oh boy!" and got down from his seat, and twisted this way and that, and wished he had some water, and wished he was at Aunt Sammy's, and was sure he was hungry and wanted his lunch. His papa and mama were thankful when the train went dashing into the depot at Boston. They were as tired and thirsty as he was, and just as dusty, and had as many ashes in their eyes.

They also had the tiredness of having a hot little boy leaning on them, asking a hundred questions, begging for water, and for food, and making himself very annoying. But they were patient because they knew whining would do no good, and because grownups know that when traveling, you must expect to be tired.

They went to a large hotel in Boston, and Mama shook off her dust and ashes, and Lou's also, and brushed Papa's coat, that looked like it was covered in sawdust, until it was black again. Then they went down to dinner, and their waiter poured each of them a glass of ice water. In those days people didn't have refrigerators in their houses, and Lou had never seen ice in the summer. He turned quickly to his papa, and cried in an excited, eager voice, "Jack Frost is in my glass, Papa!"

Chapter 8

It was too late when they reached Aunt Sammy's, for Lou to go out to see the sea or pick up shells. He was too sleepy to care, or to look at Aunt Sammy, or let her speak to him. He went right to bed with a large shell under his pillow. He could hear the murmur of the sea in it, and didn't even turn over once all night. He was so tired from the long trip, and the change to delicious sea air made him sleep soundly.

When he opened his eyes in the morning, his mama was standing by his bedside, smiling.

"What time is it? Is it morning?" he cried.

"How long have you been asleep?" asked Mama.

"About three minutes." He looked about, a little surprised. "Hey, where am I? Oh, I know now! I'm at Aunt Sammy's house, and I am going to see her ocean blue."

"Please say blue ocean," said Mama, who was quite tired of hearing him quote Aunt Sammy's poem. "Come to the window, and you can see it before you're dressed." Lou climbed up on a chair and looked out, and for the first time in his life he saw the ocean. His mama thought he would say something wonderful that she could run down and repeat to Aunt Sammy. But he didn't say a word. He was too surprised to say anything.

"It's too cold to stand in your night clothes any longer," Mama said at last. And she pulled her shawl closer around him.

"Are you cold, Mama?"

"Yes, it's very different here from the air in our little valley. Look down there. Don't you see Papa walking on the beach?"

"Oh yes!" cried Lou, clapping his hands. "Let me get dressed and go down there, too!"

Mama dressed him as fast as she could, put on a little coat and his hat, and let him go.

"Hey, Mama! I don't wear coats in summer!" he said, waiting a moment.

"You do here. Now run!"

Lou ran. He met Aunt Sammy at the foot of the stairs, but he wouldn't stop to look at her. His new uncle tried to catch him as he rushed by, but it was no use. He was off like an arrow, and soon reached his father, who was walking up and down the beach, holding his hat on, and trying to get warm.

"*I think Lou will be blown out to sea!*" Mama said to herself, as she stood at her window, watching them. "*Sweet boy, he's going to love it here!*" But before long they were blown in to breakfast, Lou's cheeks quite rosy, and both quite hungry. Lou had already picked up a few shells. It made no difference to him that they were only plain clamshells. They were the first shells he had ever found.

At the breakfast table, Aunt Sammy could see her beloved little Lou, and watch all his little ways, and laugh at all his little sayings, just as she used to do.

"What shall I give him for breakfast?" she asked. "Does he like clams?"

"He never saw a clam until now," replied his mama. "I think he had better have his usual breakfast, if you have milk to spare."

"I don't believe oatmeal and milk will satisfy him in this sharp air," said Aunt Sammy. "Lou, my love, you haven't said anything to Uncle Henry yet. This is your Uncle Henry."

"Yes, I know," said Lou. "And you're his sister." Everybody laughed at this, and Lou thought he had said something wonderful.

Chapter 9

After breakfast Lou expected to dash down to the beach again, but he had to wait until after prayers. Aunt Sammy led the way to the study, and they all followed. After a few minutes, the cook came in with a girl about twelve years old. Both of them were black. Lou had never seen anyone but white people, and he sat looking, first at one, then at the other, in perfect amazement. The moment prayers were over he ran to his mama and whispered in her ear, "Why don't they wash themselves?"

"They do wash themselves. They are as clean and nice as you or me. But God has made them with dark skin."

"Could He have made them white, if He wanted to?"

"Certainly."

"Then I wish He had. They don't look nice now."

"They *are* very nice," said Aunt Sammy, coming near them. "Martha is one of the best souls in the world. I wish I were half as good as she is. And Chloe, her little daughter, is just like her."

"But what *made* God paint them black?" asked Lou, who had quite forgotten the blue ocean, the white sand, and the shells.

"Come here, Lou," said his papa. He took Lou on his knee. "There is a country far away where all the people are like Martha and Chloe. They looked beautiful to each other, and they had never seen any white people. But one day some wicked men went there and caught a great many of them, and brought them here and sold them for money, and the people who bought them made them work very hard. Martha was one of these people, but she got away from the man who bought her and came here. You must speak kindly to her when you see her, and never let her see that you don't think she is nice. Perhaps her soul is whiter than your skin, and perhaps God loves her more than He loves me."

"Will He let her go to heaven?"

"Yes, I'm sure He will."

"Does Martha like to be black?"

"She likes to be as God made her. He loved her just as much when He gave her black skin, as He loved you when He gave you white skin."

Lou slipped down from his papa's knee and ran toward the kitchen and peeked in. He couldn't look at Martha and Chloe enough.

"There's that cute little boy peeking in!" said Chloe to her mother. "I wish I was as white as he is.

Do you think I would be white if I pulled off all my skin?"

"No, you would be as black as you are now," replied Martha, laughing. "Come in, you dear little boy! Come in and see what Martha has got for you!"

Lou stepped a little farther in, looking curiously at them both.

"My papa says you're wicked spirits from the far west!" he cried, and ran away as fast as he could.

Somehow he had gotten all that his father had said mixed up in that little head of his that was not quite three years old.

    Martha wasn't angry with him, as some foolish people would have been. She knew he was only a little boy and had made a mistake. She just laughed, and said softly to herself, "Wicked spirits! That's true[1]. And may the Lord forgive us, and make us good spirits!"

---

[1] Jeremiah17:9 The heart is deceitful above all things, and desperately wicked: who can know it?

Chapter 10

Lou ran back to the study and asked if he could go down to the shore again.

"You may go soon," said his mama. "Just as soon as I'm ready to go."

"Why do I need to wait for you, Mama? I know the way."

"Yes, but you don't know the way to keep from getting drowned. Now listen. You're never to go to the shore unless one of us is with you."

While they were talking, Aunt Sammy went into the kitchen to direct Martha about the dinner, and Martha told her what Lou had said to her.

"What a boy!" said Aunt Sammy. "I hope you don't believe Professor James said anything like that, Martha."

"Oh no, ma'am. Lors sake! no! I jist sat down and laughed until I cried."

"While he's here, I want his mama to get all the rest she can, and Chloe can take him down to the shore and watch him while he plays."

Chloe smiled. She thought it would be delightful to watch him. Everything he did seemed so amusing, and his talk was so funny. But when she went into the study and took his little white hand in her brown one, Lou looked uneasy. He pulled back his hand quickly and brushed it, as if it were dirty. His mama was ashamed of him.

"I hope you will excuse him, he is such a little fellow, and doesn't know any better. I'm sure he will like you as soon as he gets to know you better. You look so friendly and speak to him so kindly."

Chloe looked pleased, and tried once more to coax Lou to go with her, but he wouldn't.

"In a day or two he will know you better," said his mama. "I'm going to the beach soon and I can take him with me."

So Chloe went back to the kitchen to help her mother, and Lou and his mama went down to the shore. They each took a basket, and while Lou picked up shells and pebbles, mama searched for sea mosses. There were some lovely kinds to be found here. She didn't find many on the beach today, however. When she saw some rocks a little ways off, she thought she would go and look in the crevices among them, and see if any had gotten caught there when the waves came up. She drew a line in the sand with her parasol, and said to Lou, "Look here, Lou! You must not go past this line while I'm gone. I am going to search for mosses among the rocks, just a little way off. Now be sure not to go any nearer the water than this line."

"Why not, Mama?"

"Because it's dangerous."

"She walked away slowly, looking back every moment or two, to see that Lou was obeying her.

He was busy collecting shells, a good way from the water.

"*He's quite safe,*" she said to herself. "*I don't have to watch him so closely. He'll stay back from the waves.*" She went a little farther, and among the rocks found tiny pools of water, full of mosses. Some were green, some pink, some pure white. She gave a cry of surprise and pleasure.

"How beautiful! Little gardens full of sea flowers! Come here, Lou!" she called, "Come and see some lovely little gardens made of water!"

But Lou didn't hear her. The wind carried her voice another way and the waves were splashing and making a lot of noise. She stooped down and with the end of her parasol, fished out some of the green seaweeds and graceful mosses. They lay in little heaps on her hand, and didn't look at all like they did in the water. Even though they weren't as pretty, she thought she would take them home. Meanwhile Lou wandered about. When he saw a large, beautiful white stone, just beyond the line his mama had marked, he ran to get it.

"*It's only a little way past the line; Mama won't care,*" he thought.

He then saw a shell a little farther off. It was bright yellow. "There's a shell that looks just like a little chicken!" he cried. "Mama will be glad when she sees my little chicken-shell." So he went on, step by step, nearer the sea, and the whole time, the sea was coming nearer to him.

Chapter 11

"I'M GOING TO run and jump on that little boy's back and give him a good soak!" said a small wave to its mother, the great ocean.

"Oh no! You would frighten him," said the mother. Then the little wave ran back into her arms, and meant to be a good little wave and do just as she said. But it was full of mischief that morning, and somehow it ran back again and came close to Lou, and oh, how it wanted to jump up and splash all over him! But once more it ran back, and hid by its mother.

Lou stooped down to look at something odd upon the shore. It looked like a piece of white jelly as it lay there. If he could have seen it in the sea where it belonged, he would have seen something like a little fairy umbrella, that kept opening and shutting, and floating about, more delicate than anything made of silver. It was a jellyfish.

"I'll carry this home," said Lou. And just then, the little wave, that was so full of fun that it couldn't help it, saw Lou stooping down as if on purpose. It ran and jumped right over his head, wetting him all over.

Lou lost his breath, and though he opened his mouth wide, he couldn't scream for a moment or two. When the scream did come it frightened the little wave so that it scampered back to its mother, terrified half out of its wits, and Lou's mama felt her heart stop beating, and all her strength leaving her. She threw down her basket and her mosses, and ran toward the spot where she had left Lou. He came shrieking toward her, quite wild with terror, while his hat and his basket floated comfortably off to sea.

A young woman, sitting on the shore with a baby in her arms, saw the whole thing. She couldn't help laughing, but she came forward, good-naturedly, and said to Lou's mama, "You never can carry that heavy boy, ma'am. You look ready to drop, yourself.

If you'll take my baby, I'll carry your little boy to my house, and we'll change his wet clothes. I live close by."

"Thank you, you're very kind. But we live nearby too, and we had better go home. I've been scared out of my wits, and can hardly stand."

Aunt Sammy sat at her window, with her sewing in her hand. She heard several fearful screams and looking out, saw her sister come panting along with a baby in her arms, while a stranger followed behind carrying Lou, kicking and struggling, in hers. She ran down and met them in the hall.

"What *is* the matter with Lou?" she cried. "I would think a shark had bitten off one of his legs!"

"Oh Sammy, he's as wet as he can be!" said Mama, "and I've been frightened half to death! Help get off his clothes; he's shivering!"

Hearing the noise, Martha and Chloe came running to the door, and Martha grabbed Lou and carried him out to the kitchen, where there was a fire burning. With all of them helping, his wet clothes were taken off and he was dried and calmed down. At last he stopped crying, and instead used his mouth to eat a little cookie that Chloe slipped into his hand. His mama brought down some dry clothes, and he felt as well as ever, except that his cheeks were nearly roasted by the fire.

By this time his mama was so tired that she had to lie down, and she told Lou he must do one of two things: go and lie down with her, or stay with Chloe. He didn't want to do either, but he was in a humble state of mind after his dunking, and didn't feel like arguing. He said he would stay with Chloe.

"Take him out to the front of the house, where it's warm and sunny," said Martha.

"But he has lost his hat," said Chloe. "He will get sunburned."

"Then make him a cap of paper, honey."

"Yes, I will!" said Chloe. "A little soldier's cap." She found a newspaper, folded it, put in a pin or two, and made a paper feather in a twinkling. Lou watched her, trembling with delight, and as soon as it was done, he began to march up and down in front of the house, feeling a lot more like a man than he had since his dunking.

Chapter 12

AFTER DINNER HIS papa went out to get a hat to replace the one Lou lost. While he was gone Lou knelt in a chair at the window and looked out at the ocean, while his mama and Aunt Sammy sat with their books and work, sometimes talking, sometimes reading.

"You will be able to trust Lou anywhere on the beach after this," said Aunt Sammy. "The fright he has had today will be a good lesson for him."

"I don't think he deserves to go there again, after his disobedience," said his mama.

"I don't want to go there anymore," said Lou, turning quickly around.

"You shouldn't say that," replied Mama, "you know it's not true."

"I don't and I don't; and I know the reason why I don't."

"Perhaps he is afraid of getting wet again," said Aunt Sammy.

"I hope he's not afraid of that," said Mama. "Well, Lou. Why don't you want to go to the beach again?" Lou was silent.

"Ah! He *is* afraid," said Aunt Sammy.

"You would be afraid too if the big ocean came and drowned you," said Lou.

"You weren't drowned, you were only splashed," said his mama. Lou was silent again. He had made up his mind never to set foot on the shore, but he didn't want Mama to think he was a coward.

"I wish Papa would come with my new hat," he said at last. "Then I could go for a walk with Chloe. Chloe says she'll take me to see lots of shops, and let me look in all the windows."

"It's too far for you to walk to town so late in the afternoon," said Aunt Sammy. "I'm surprised that Chloe thought of such a thing."

"Then what *can* I do? Mama wouldn't let me bring my kitty, or my hatchet, or my wheelbarrow. I don't have anything to play with."

"Say Mama *couldn't*, not Mama *wouldn't*," said Papa, coming into the room with the new hat.

The next morning, soon after breakfast, Chloe came to take Lou out. His aunt gave him a basket, since he had lost his own. Papa brought out the little wooden shovel, which had been hidden away until now. But Lou refused to go to the beach, while he looked joyfully at the shovel and held out his hand for it.

"You can't have the shovel unless you go to the beach," said his papa. "It's only good for digging in the soft sand."

Lou began to cry. Mama urged, and Aunt Sammy coaxed, and Uncle Henry argued with him; but it did no good.

"You wouldn't have gotten wet if you had not disobeyed me," said Mama. "Today you will only go where you're allowed, and nothing will harm you."

"The blue ocean will run after me," said Lou, with a finger in each eye.

"And you can run away from the blue ocean," said Aunt Sammy. "Come, we're all going. You don't want to stay at home without us, do you?"

"I don't want to be wet," persisted Lou, and he started to cry.

"But you won't get wet this time. You got wet yesterday because you went too near the water," said Uncle Henry.

"The water is cold!" said Lou. "And it tastes terrible. And it gets in my ears and my eyes," he kept on crying, sadly.

"We'll go without him," said Papa. "Come, Laura. Come, Sammy. Let's go." He thought that when Lou saw them all going, he would want to go too. But he was wrong. Lou stayed behind with Chloe and sat down on the stairs and cried his heart out.

Chapter 13

"What are we going to do, William?" asked Lou's mama, as soon as they got out of hearing. "Should we *make* him go, even though he's afraid?"

"No, I think we had better not say anything more to him, and he will probably be eager to go as soon as he sees we have stopped urging him." So they all had a charming walk, gathering seaweeds, shells and other things, and now and then stopping to sit on the rocks to look at the beautiful waves that came running in, white with foam. When they got home Aunt Sammy showed her sister how to arrange her seaweeds. Lou looked on with great interest, and wished he could do some of this pretty work. His mama gave him a bit of moss, and he let it float as she did hers, in clear water. Then he caught it on a piece of white paper, and spread it out with a pin. This kept him busy and happy until dinnertime. After dinner Uncle Henry said he was going into town, and would take Lou with him if his mama thought the walk wouldn't be too long for him. She hesitated a little.

"Mrs. Brown, who has a cottage near ours, lets her little children go to town," said Aunt Sammy. "I don't think the walk will hurt him." Lou was very glad to hear that, and to see his mama's smile of consent. He marched off by his uncle's side with the air of a prince. His uncle looked down at his little companion proudly.

"*He is a handsome boy!*" he thought. As they walked on, Lou asked questions almost without stopping, and said so many amusing things that his uncle thought he had never had a more pleasant walk to town. When they reached it, they went into several shops. First they went to a toyshop, and Uncle Henry asked to see some little boats. He was shown a good many, and at last he chose one painted in red and white stripes, with snowy sails, and a little flag flying at the masthead. Lou smiled and his heart beat when he saw this little ship. He knew it must be for him, and yet that seemed too good to be true.

"Tomorrow we will go to a pond near my house and sail this little ship," said Uncle Henry.

"Whose ship is it?" asked Lou.

"It's mine now, but I am going to give it to the first boy I see who looks like a good boy." Lou ran a little way ahead of his uncle, and stood in his path.

"Do I look like a good boy?" he asked.

"Yes, I really think you do. I suppose I'll have to give it to you then. What will you call it?"

"I'll call it mine."

"No, what name will you give it, I mean? Every ship has a name of its own, did you know that?"

"No, Uncle. I'll call it—I'll call it—I don't know what to call it."

"We'll have to let your mama name it then. Carry it carefully. Is it too heavy?"

"Oh no, Uncle. I could carry it if it was a hundred times as big as a man." Just then they came to a candy shop. Lou stopped to look at the nice things displayed in the windows. A tall, pale man, who saw his little eager face from the inside of the shop, came out.

"You have a fine little boy there," he said.

"He's my little nephew," said Uncle Henry.

"Oh, I thought he was your son," said the man. "But it's all the same, Mr. Gray. Why don't you bring him in and let's see if he likes sweet things. Here, my little fellow. Here is some candy for you."

Lou took the little package the man handed him, and while his uncle and the shopkeeper talked, he ate as fast as he could. After a while his uncle said, "Don't eat any more, Lou. I don't think your mama will like you eating so much."

"Yes, she lets me eat all I want," said Lou.

"I doubt that. Don't eat any more now, anyway. We'll see what she says when we get home."

Lou instantly forgot how kind his uncle had been, and became very angry. "You're a mean

uncle!" he shouted, while large tears rolled down his cheeks. "A bad, naughty, wicked uncle!"

"I hope you'll excuse this angry little boy," said his uncle, not knowing what to do. He didn't want to go through the streets with a child screaming in anger. The shopkeeper said at last, "Come into my shop until the boy calms down. I'll give him some ice cream."

"*I guess I'll have to do that, or he'll never stop,*" thought his uncle. "*I'm sorry I brought him with me. I'll never take him with me again.*" He led Lou into the shop, and two plates of ice cream were placed before them. Lou stopped crying. He had never eaten any ice cream, but he *knew* this must be something good. He took a spoonful, and it was wonderful. Then he jumped down from his seat, and ran and threw his arms around his uncle, and looked up in his face with a sweet smile.

"Do you love me, Uncle Henry?" he asked. Uncle Henry couldn't help loving him. So Lou went back to his seat, and ate his ice cream in peace.

Chapter 14

THE NEXT DAY Lou's papa said he was going to go swimming in the ocean, and suggested that Mama go with him. "I want Lou to go in the water too," said Mama. When Lou heard this, he let out one of his terrible screams.

"Okay," said Papa, "You don't have to go. You're a foolish little boy and don't know what is good for you. We'll have a wonderful time in the water, and so would you, if you made up your mind to try it."

"I'll take care of him while you're gone," said Aunt Sammy, "or he may go with Chloe to watch you play in the water."

"I'd rather stay with Aunt Sammy," said Lou.

"Then when your papa and mama go, you may come to my room. That is, you may come if you're going to be pleasant."

"I *am* going to be pleasant," said Lou. In about an hour, his aunt heard a gentle little knock at her door.

"Come in!" she said. Lou came in. "Now," said Aunt Sammy, "what shall I do to amuse you?

Do you want me to tell you stories, or should I let you play with my little tea set?"

"I like both best," said Lou.   His aunty laughed.

"I'll tell the stories first, then." She told him two quite long ones; they amused him so much that he laughed until the tears rolled down his cheeks, and he got up several times to stamp and dance.

His aunty found it very amusing to tell stories to a boy who enjoyed it so much, but after finishing the second, she said she was tired. She went to her closet, and took down a tiny little tea set that she put down in front of Lou, with some water, a few crackers, and some very small lumps of sugar.

"You have to make what I give you last a long time," she said, "because your mama won't like it if I let you have more. You can pour yourself as many cups of tea as you want, and put in sugar as long as it lasts."

Lou sat down on the stool, having a chair for a table. Aunt Sammy took a book and began to read. When she had read about an hour, she looked at Lou to see what he was doing, and found him still quite happy with his little cups of tea.

"How easy it is to keep him busy playing!" she thought. "I've never seen a better child. What can make Laura say he is so troublesome?"

She had finished her book, and now took out her work. She was going to bind two blankets with red ribbon.

"What are you doing, Aunty?" asked Lou, who had used up all his tea.

"I am going to bind these blankets."

"What is binding?"

"Come here and see. I put the ribbon all along the edge like this; then I fasten it with stitches, like this."

"Why do you bind it?"

"To make it look pretty."

"I wouldn't think you would care whether your blankets looked pretty or not."

"Well, I do care," said Aunt Sammy.

"Do you get up in the night and light the candle, and look at your blankets?" asked Lou.

"Oh you little chatterbox, you're as full of questions as you can hold. I see your papa and mama coming up from the beach. Papa has the swimsuits in a green pail, and Mama has the wet towels. Listen! Come and hide under this blanket and see what Mama says when she doesn't see you."

Lou crept under like lightning. Soon Mama came in and threw herself into the first chair.

"Oh, I'm so tired!" she cried.

"Did you have fun?" asked Aunt Sammy.

"Yes, it was wonderful. The waves came in as fast as they could, and dashed over us wonderfully. I've worn myself out with so much fun and laughter."

"I'm very glad you enjoy going in the ocean so much," said Aunt Sammy. "I'm sure it will do you good, and William too. I think your appetite has improved since you came here."

"Yes, it has," said Mama.

At this moment, Lou, who had been silently waiting for her to ask where he was, came rushing out from his hiding place where he had been nearly smothered, and threw himself on his mama and began beating her with all his might.

"You naughty Mama! You didn't say, 'Where is my little Lou?' You don't love me at all!"

"Oh, Laura, I see you're right," said Aunt Sammy, "in saying you don't know what to do with such a child. Oh Lou, how *can* you be so naughty to your poor delicate mama?"

"I want her to love me!" sobbed Lou.

"You have a very odd way of making her love you then."

Meanwhile, Lou's mama rose wearily from her seat.

"I suppose I'll have to punish him," she said, "though it never does any good."

"He ought to be punished, certainly," said his aunt.

Lou was led away to his mama's room. After a time she came back to Aunt Sammy's room.

"I am very sorry for you, Laura," said her sister. "Lou *can* be the sweetest and best child in the world. I've had a delightful morning with him."

"Yes, but that makes it even harder when he has one of his tantrums," said his Mama.

Chapter 15

ALL THE NEXT day Lou was in disgrace. His food was placed on a little table in a corner, and he had to eat it all alone. His papa and mama spoke to him very seldom, and then seriously and sadly. He moped around the house, not knowing what to do. His heart felt like a lump of lead. At last he went to Aunt Sammy's room.

"You can come in, Lou," she said, "but I have no stories to tell you today. This is the second time in your little life that you have hit your dear, precious mama, who loves you so much."

"I never hit her before this," said Lou in a sullen voice.

"Yes, you did. I was with you at the time. Your papa was driving us in the sleigh. You were sitting on your mama's lap, and I was by her side. The sleigh tipped over and we were all thrown out into the snow. You instantly flew at your poor mama and hit her. You thought she had thrown you into the snow on purpose. You were a very little boy then, and I thought you didn't know any better." Lou was silent. He sat kicking his heels against his chair, feeling very unhappy indeed.

"I know what I would do, if I were you," continued Aunt Sammy. "I would go away into some little corner where no one could see me, and I would ask God to forgive me, and beg him to make me good."

"Papa said just the same thing," said Lou, and he stopped kicking.

"Yes, and he and your mama pray for you day and night." Lou got up and sauntered around the room. All his best friends were unhappy with him. No one had kissed him that day. And ever since he could remember, he had been loved and caressed so much that he never thought any more of the love his friends gave him than he did of the air God gave him to breathe.

Finally he walked softly away. He knew of a place where he could go and hide his sorrowful little heart away, and pray to God to forgive him and help him fight against his fiery temper. There was a large lilac bush in Aunt Sammy's little garden, and underneath it there was room to crawl in. Chloe had shown it to him. He went there now, and folded his hands; the same hands that had tried to hurt his dear mama, and would have hurt her if they had been large and strong enough. He folded his hands, but he didn't know what to say. But God saw the little sad face hidden away under the lilac bush, and the little heavy, sorrowful heart.[2] He knew that Lou wished he had not been so naughty. He knew that he longed to be forgiven. And he did forgive him.[3]

After a while Lou crawled out from his little hideout, and went softly up to his mama's room. He didn't have to tell her how sorry he was, or to ask her forgiveness. She saw it in his face. She opened her arms, and he ran and threw himself into them and clasped his around her neck, and burst into a flood of tears. His mama cried too. But after a little while she wiped away her tears and his, and they talked about being good until they both thought there was nothing else in the world worth caring about.

---

[2] You know my sitting down and my rising up; You understand my thought afar off. Psalms 139:2
Before a word is on my tongue you, LORD, know it completely. Psalms 139:4 NIV

[3] If we confess our sins, he is faithful and just and will forgive us our sins and purify us from all unrighteousness. NIV

Chapter 16

AFTER THIS EVENT, which was like a cleansing rain shower, Lou became a little piece of sunshine. He was so sweet and pleasant that no one could help loving him. His mama made him repeat to her the poem about "My Mother,"[4] which she had taught him long ago, and which now seemed to have a new meaning for him. "Hey!" he exclaimed, "are you the same mother that 'on my cheeks sweet kisses pressed'? Is this the arm I used to lie on when I was a baby? Oh, then I'll always try to be, 'affectionate and kind to thee, who was so very kind to me!'"

Since he had now made up his mind to control himself, he no longer objected to going to the beach and his mama had free time to wander off by herself, or to sit quietly in her room, looking out at the ocean, or enjoying the sight of her special little boy, as he made wells in the sand with Chloe by his side, and ran all around as happy as the breeze. These last weeks at the seaside were very happy weeks, and they all grew quite strong and well.

But at last vacation was over, and they had to go home. And when they got there, home looked

---

[4] See Appendix for words to this poem, *My Mother*.

very pleasant. Lou ran about joyfully to all the places he loved best, and was very glad to see his kitty once more, and to play with his little hatchet and wheelbarrow. It was now time for Mama to begin to get ready for winter. Apples were peeled and cored and strung, and hung up to dry. Tomatoes and peaches were canned, and put away in the storeroom. The beautiful little red and yellow crabapples were picked and made into jelly, and the jelly was poured into glasses, and bits of white paper pasted over each.

Papa had his share of work, too. Besides teaching at the university, he had a lot to do gathering in the fruit from the orchard. The apples and the winter pears were picked carefully, and stored away in the cellar. A little later, pumpkins and squashes and other vegetables were brought in from the field, and stored away with the apples. Then the potatoes needed to be dug, and piled up in heaps all over the field, and then collected in baskets, which were emptied into carts, and a big bin in the cellar was filled with them.

Lou watched many of these activities, and tried to be a great help. He wheeled home a pumpkin in his wheelbarrow, and several loads of potatoes. Meanwhile he was learning something new every day, because his papa kept him with him a lot of the time in the orchard and out in the field, and was constantly teaching him the names of things and their uses.

Before long there was a sharp frost that took everybody by surprise. Mama hurried to get her tender plants into the shelter of her little greenhouse that opened out of the study on one side, and the dining room on the other. Many of the flowers died, and some only died down to the ground. Their roots lay sheltered underground, all ready to send up new leaves in the spring. Lou followed his mama around, chattering like a squirrel. "Look at this picture, Mama," he said. "Papa just gave it to me."

"Yes, dear, I see," said Mama, and she went on arranging her plants on the shelves. It was a picture of a little dog in a cage with a lion.

"Why doesn't the lion eat the little dog? Would he eat me, if I were there? Would he kiss me?"

"I don't think he would kiss you," said Mama, "because he doesn't know you."

"But if I would tell him my name was Lou James, what would he do then? Would he say, "Well —w-e-l-l!" in a roaring voice? He couldn't say it in a soft voice, could he, Mama?"

"Oh, I don't know," she answered, laughing. "You do ask so many odd questions, Lou, and I'm *so* busy!"

"I only want to ask one more, Mama. When I am beginning to die, will my eyes be blazed?"

"Blazed?" repeated Mama, setting down the flowerpot she held in her hands.

"Yes, blazed. Papa told me a story about a dog whose eyes were blazed when he lay dying."

"*Glazed* he said."

"Yes, glazed, that's it. And what shall I be put in when I die? Will wicked soldiers that are buried in the ground get me? Will God give me a new soul, then? Will I come right up out of the ground the minute the trumpet sounds?[5]"

"My dear Lou," said Mama, "God will teach you what to do, when the time comes. After you die, and your body is laid away in the ground, he will watch over it wherever it is, and keep it safely. You don't need to worry about it. He loves you even more than Papa and Mama love you." Lou now ran away to play, quite satisfied.

"*Ah!*" thought his mama, looking after him. "*I could spend all my time answering his questions!*" Just then he came running back.

"What's a dragon, Mama? Does he drag?"

"Who has been talking to you about dragons?"

---

[5] For the Lord Himself will descend from heaven with a shout, with the voice of an archangel, and with the trumpet of God. And the dead in Christ will rise first.
1 Thessalonians 4:16

"Nobody. I heard Papa read in the Bible at prayers about a great red dragon that had seven heads, and ten horns, and ten crowns on his heads."[6]

"Then if you heard about it from Papa you had better ask him whatever you want to know. As for me, I've never seen a dragon, and never want to see one. Now sweetheart, please don't ask me another question right now."

---

[6] Then I stood on the sand of the sea. And I saw a beast rising up out of the sea, having seven heads and ten horns, and on his horns ten crowns, and on his heads a blasphemous name. Revelation 13:1

Chapter 17

Quite early in the winter, Lou was sitting in a high chair near the window, when his papa came in from the Post Office with the letters and papers. One letter was from Uncle Henry. Mama read it to herself first, and then she ran to Lou and kissed him and said, "God has sent a little baby to Aunt Sammy. It's your cousin, and I hope you will love her very much."

"It's a girl, and her name is Sammy, named after her mama."

"How did God get her to Aunt Sammy?" asked Lou. "Did she come flying softly down like a snowflake? How funny it would look to see a lot of little babies all flying down together!"

"If they were, I'd go out and catch one," said Mama. "I would catch a little sister for you. Aunt Sammy sends her love to you, and says she wishes you could see her baby."

"Can I go there?" cried Lou, jumping down from his chair.

"Not today. I hope Aunt Sammy will bring her here next spring."

"Well," he said in a joyful voice. "And I'll let her use my little hatchet."

"Oh, girls don't like hatchets."

"Do they like wheelbarrows?"

"Not much."

"What sort of things *are* girls, then? I don't think they have much sense."

"Little girls are usually quieter than boys. They like to play with dolls, and pretend they are real babies."

"I am glad *I'm* not a girl!"

"Sometimes I wish you *were* a girl. You're so noisy on the stairs, and you slam the doors so hard, and frighten me by climbing up into such dangerous places."

"I *will* be a little girl then," said Lou, climbing into his mama's lap. "But you'll have to give me a new name, and buy me a dolly."

"Ok. Your name is Mary. As for a doll, here's one that I was going to give your cousin Ella, at Christmas. Do you want to play with that, my dear little Mary?"

"Yes please, Mama," said 'Mary,' in a soft voice. He sat down and held the doll the best he could, but he didn't know how to act. "I wish my baby would behave," he said. "She falls over as soon as I let go of her. I think I'll give her a ride in my wheelbarrow."

"Oh, you don't have any wheelbarrow now that you're a little girl," said Mama.

Then I'll toss her up in the air. People always toss up babies. It says so, in stories."

"But they don't toss them up to the ceiling, as you do. That would hurt them. They just pretend to toss them up."

Just then Abigail called Mama and she went to talk to her. Lou picked up the doll and looked at her

closely. "*I wonder what she's made of inside?*" he thought. "*I'll prick her to see if any blood comes out.*

Hmm, the pin won't go in! Well, I can crack her open with my hatchet, and then I'll know!" He ran for his hatchet, and with one blow crushed the doll's head to powder, because it was made of porcelain. His mama came back just in time to see what he had done."

"That was wrong! You know I don't like you to destroy your toys, Lou."

"Oh, I'm Lou again! I'm so glad! I don't like to be a little Mary, at all. I didn't break the doll for mischief, I only wanted to see what she had inside of her."

"Gather up the pieces and carry them away," said his mama. "I am sorry I gave you your little cousin's doll. It would have lasted her a year! I hoped it would be fun to play with and keep you out of mischief long enough for me to write to Aunt Sammy. Now I don't know what to do with you."

"I'll sit still, Mama. You can write a letter as long as from here to Uncle Arthur's."

Mama sat down to write, and Lou played about the room, amusing himself. Once when his mama looked up, she saw him unroll a piece of ribbon, and stretch it across the floor. "There! That is the Jordan River," he said. "It flows through the land of Canaan. I wish I had some Israelites. Let me see! That old doll would have worked for one." His mama went on with her letter. At last it was finished. She closed her desk and sat down with her sewing work. One of her spools rolled from her lap, and ran across the room on the other side of Lou's river.

"Get my spool for me, Lou," she said.

"I would, Mama, but I'll have to wet my feet in the Jordan River."

"Ok. I can use another one. I hope your Jordan River will dry up before long, because I don't want to wet *my* feet crossing it."

"Its waves will roll back at my command," replied Lou. "Look, Mama!" And he began to roll up the piece of tape with a manner that seemed to say, "Moses himself couldn't have done better!"

Part 3

Chapter 1

One day when Lou was almost four years old, he came home from his uncle's where he had spent the morning, and found his mama busy packing a trunk.

"Oh, whose trunk is that? Are we going anywhere?" he cried. "How soon are we going? Will we stay long?"

"Which question should I answer first, you little curious cat?" asked Mama. "To make a long story short, I'll tell you that Papa is going to Boston, nobody else is going, and he will be gone a week or so."

"Can't I go with him?"

"Oh no," said his papa. "I need you to stay and take care of Mama. You have to tell her stories and not let her miss me." Lou didn't know that his papa was kidding. He thought Papa really meant that he had to take care of his mama. So when Papa had kissed them goodbye, Lou said to Mama, "I am growing up quite fast. It will be my birthday next July, and it's March now. I won't let anything hurt you while Papa is away. You don't need to be a bit afraid." His mama smiled and said she was sure he would take good care of her.

After a while it began to grow dark. Lou knew his mama couldn't see well enough to sew anymore that day. During the day, they had sunshine to light up their house and work by, but at night, they only had candles and oil lamps, which don't make as much light as a light bulb.

"Papa always reads to you in the evening," he said. "I'll do that too." He climbed up and took down a book, and began to read. It was only pretend, for he didn't know one letter. First he read the story of Joseph, with so much animation that his mama really enjoyed it.

"Now I'll sing to you." He sang a hymn he had often heard his papa sing, which said something about a "great load of sin." He stopped singing and seemed to be thinking.

"What are you thinking about?" asked his mama at last.

"I was wondering what a load of sin is. Is it a load of gravel?"

"I am glad you asked me, if you didn't know better than that. Sin is not obeying God. Don't you remember the bundle Christian had on his back? That was his load of sin."[7]

---

[7] Christian is the main character in *Pilgrim's Progress* by John Bunyan

"I hope I'll never have one on my back," said Lou, looking over his shoulder.

"Then you must begin now, while you're a little boy, to do nothing that you know is wrong."

"I will," said Lou. "And now Mama, I'll tell you a story. There was a boy who piled up wood for his father until it toushed the sky."

"Touched, not toushed," said Mama.

"Touched the sky. Then he climbed up on it and touched the sky, himself."

"How did it feel?" asked his mama.

"Oh, it felt like stars, all over."

"And how did the stars feel?"

"Oh, they felt bright and sunny. That's all I know about the boy. Was that a good story, Mama? Did you like it? Am I taking good care of you?"

"Yes, you're taking excellent care of me. I'll tell Papa all about it when he comes home."

"When you lie on the sofa after dinner, I'll cover you up, just as Papa does. If you shut your eyes you'll think I *am* Papa."

His mama smiled and kissed him. "I think you had better go and play, now," she said.

"But you will be all alone."

"I like to be alone, sometimes."

"Okay, but call me as soon as you feel lonely and I'll come right in." So Lou ran to play, feeling very happy indeed.

Chapter 2

"Mama," he said, running back in a few minutes, "I wish Papa was at home. I want to ask him if it's going to rain. Abigail says if it's going to rain, she doesn't want to hang her clothes out."

"Papa couldn't tell for sure, what the weather will be. I think that it *is* going to rain."

"But Papa knows everything. He's a proph."

"A prophet, you mean?"

"Yes, a prophet, that's it."

"What do you mean?" exclaimed Mama. "There are no prophets these days."

"Then why do people call Papa a proph?"

"Oh, I see now!" said Mama, laughing. "Papa's close friends call him 'The Prof.' which means 'The Professor.' They don't mean that he is a prophet."

Lou looked disappointed. "Well, even if he can't tell what's *going* to happen, he knows all that *has* happened," he said. "He's told me all the stories in the Bible and stories about Indians and stories about shipwrecks. He knows the names of all the plants that grow around here and the names of the stars."

"Your papa does knows a lot," replied mama, "but he won't tell you that he knows everything. The more people know the less they think they know."

"Jacob is out in the garden," said Lou, "and he says his father knows more than my father. And I told him Papa was a proph."

"You and Jacob argue too much."

"Well, Jacob always keeps saying his house is better than my house, and his mama's better than my mama."

"Let him say so then, if it makes him feel any better. Besides, his house *is* better than this and his mama is as good as she can be. Now don't let me hear of any more quarrels. The next time Jacob says he lives in the best house, say 'Yes, you do,' and that will end it."

"But I don't want him to live in the best house."

"I don't see how you can help it, unless you go and burn it down. The truth is, you ought to be two of the best boys in the world, with such wise and good men for your fathers."

Lou went off, feeling quite discouraged, and he and Jacob kept on arguing about one thing after another until they got quite tired of each other.

"I'm going home, you old Lou," said Jacob.

"Good, I'm glad, you old Jacob. I guess you wouldn't act like that if your father had told you about the great red dragon with seven heads and ten horns and seven crowns on his heads."

"Oh, what was it?" asked Jacob, coming back.

"I'm not telling you any more. You don't even know what a dragon is."

"My father will tell me. My father knows more than yours does!" Before Lou had time to answer, Jacob ran off as fast as his feet could carry him.

"*After this I'll stay home and play with Joshua,*" he said to himself. "*Joshua and I have the same father and live in the same house, so we have nothing to quarrel about.*"

When Lou went into the house, dinner was ready. He sat in his papa's seat and tried to amuse his mama with his conversation.

"Mama, I saw a toad in the garden and tried to catch him. I got my hand on him once, but he got away."

"How did the toad feel when you put your hand on him?"

"He felt hoppy."

"I will tell you something else. Papa says there once was a little boy who had a big, good dog. One day the boy fell in the water, and the good dog jumped in and pulled him right out. Where do good dogs go when they die?"

"Some people think they go to heaven. What do you think?"

Lou smiled and didn't answer. At last he said, "I think they go down into the ground and stay there."

"So do I," said Mama.

Chapter 3

After dinner Mama said that since Lou had tried so hard to entertain her, she was now going to entertain him by reading a short story. She went into the study, and took down a little book from one of the upper shelves, and after looking through the pages a little while, she said she would read about a boy named Lewis.

"Am I the boy?" asked Lou.

"No, this Lewis does not spell his name the same as yours. Yours is L-O-U-I-S and this boy is L-E-W-I-S. Let's see if he's like you at all."

Little Lewis was a smart boy, but he was not a good boy, for he was always contradicting. If his father said, "Lewis, your face is not clean," Lewis would answer, "My face *is* clean!" And when his father said, "Lewis, you always contradict," he said, "I *never* contradict."

Once Lewis lay upon the sofa, which was covered with beautiful satin. Lewis had his feet on the sofa, and rolled around on it with his shoes on. There was a soft pillow at the head of the sofa. Lewis turned over, and put his feet on the pillow.

His father soon saw what he was doing, and he cried out, "Lewis! Lewis! What are you doing?" Then Lewis turned around quickly, and lay properly on the sofa. But his father went on, "Haven't I forbidden you to lie on the sofa like that at least twenty times? You are not to roll around on the sofa with your shoes on."

Lewis replied, "I'm not rolling on the sofa."

"What!" said his father, "You deny it? Didn't I just see you with your feet on the cushion?"

"But I don't have my feet on it now," said Lewis.

"That's true, but they were there a moment ago, and you knew it was forbidden."

"No, I didn't know it was forbidden," said Lewis.

"Then if you have such a bad memory, I'll have to do something to strengthen it." And his father took a little rod, and punished Lewis. Then he said, "Now remember, you're not to put your feet on the sofa cushion. If you do it again, I'll have to punish you again."

Lewis didn't do it again, but he contradicted as much as ever. If he couldn't find anyone else to contradict, he would argue with himself in the most silly way. Sometimes he would say, "A dog is not a dog; the black stone is not black; people do not eat; a naughty boy is not a naughty boy" and foolish things like that. Finally his father said that a child who was always contradicting wouldn't be allowed to talk at all. He made him go and stand in the corner, and not speak a word. This was a great punishment, for Lewis liked to talk. But it didn't cure him. He was good for a couple of hours after he came out of the corner, but then he forgot all about it, and contradicted as much as ever."

"Is that all?" asked Lou.

"Yes, that is all. Do you know any boy at all like Lewis?"

"Yes, I know Jacob." His mama smiled.

"I know a lot of boys like him," she said. "And one of them plays with Jacob."

Lou looked down. He knew who the little boy was.

Chapter 4

WHEN LOU'S PAPA came back from Boston he brought several large cards with pictures of animals on them. Beneath each animal there were some words in large print. His papa thought he could learn to read with these cards. Lou was very much pleased with his cards. There were twelve of them. He had never seen such large, colored pictures of animals before. He made the cards stand all around the dining room, leaning against chairs, and then he pretended to neigh like a horse, and bray like a donkey, and roar like a lion.

"I wish I knew what kind of a noise a camel makes," he said. "I suppose it's a humpy kind of a noise."

"I hope you will learn to read, now that you have these big, beautiful cards," said his mama. "You're now four and a half years old, and don't even know your letters.

"I am six years old," said Lou." Half of four is two, and four and two makes six."

"What nonsense! But you do know some math!" said Mama, laughing and patting his little curly head. "You want to learn to read, don't you?" she asked.

"No, I am going to be a dunce. But I will know some things, even if I don't learn to read. I already know some things now, things that I've seen." He picked up his kitty, and began to swing her about.

"Don't do that; you'll hurt Kitty," said Mama.

"Does that hurt you, kittybam, kittybas, kittybat?" asked Lou.

"Now I do wonder where you picked that up!" cried his mama.

"I didn't pick it up anywhere. I said it myself."

"He probably heard some of his uncle's boys studying their Latin grammar," said his papa.

"Yes, I did. Arthur kept saying 'eram, eras, erat,' until it got stuck in my head like a nail. He didn't say kittybam, kittybas, kittybat, though. I said that." He ran out to the wood house, and began to turn the wheel of his papa's lathe. After a long time, his mama, thinking he must be tired, went out to speak to him.

"Aren't you tired, Lou?" she asked. "You could come in now, and play with your picture cards again."

"No, Mama, I'd rather turn the wheel, because it's more exercise."

"I am afraid you're working too hard."

"That doesn't matter. If I am going to be a dunce, I'll have to work hard for my living."

"Who says so?"

"Papa. He says that when dunces grow up, all they are fit for is to work building railroads and digging wells."

"Yes," said Mama, "and when you grow up to be a man, it won't be very pleasant to be hewing stones or drawing water in dirty, patched clothes, while Papa and I live in this nice house, and wear clean and whole clothes. Of course you won't be fit to sit at our table, and you won't be interested in the things we talk about. You get by now without knowing how to read, because I read to you so much, and Papa tells you so many stories."

"Can't you read to me when I'm a big man?"

"No, you won't have time to listen to reading. You'll have to be working in ditches to earn your own living." Lou began to look serious.

"I'll come right in and learn to read this very minute," he said.

"Okay. I'll be glad to teach you."

But learning to read requires patience, and Lou had no patience. He grew whiny and grumpy, and couldn't see the letters; his eyes were so full of tears.

"I won't teach you if you behave this way," said his mama. "Go away to your own little room, and ask God to forgive you for being so impatient, and help you to focus on your lesson." Lou went. When he came back, he was quite pleasant again.

"I prayed six times," he said, "and that is as much as I thought was necessary."

Chapter 5

ONE SUNDAY MORNING Lou's mama dressed him very nicely for church, and read to him for a long time. "Now may I go downstairs and sit in my little carriage, until it's time for church?" he asked.

"Yes, you may go if you'll be very quiet and not disturb Papa."

Lou promised to be quiet, and ran joyfully down to the wood house, where a wicker carriage was kept, the same carriage he used when a he was a baby. His mama took her Bible, and sat down in her room to read. It was a beautiful day, early in October, almost as warm as a summer morning. She felt very happy as she sat in her pleasant room, free from care and trouble. She read a few verses, and then she laid down her book, and began to think of Lou.

"*Oh, will he grow up to be a good and useful man?*" she thought. "*He is so intelligent, he has such a good memory, he is so full of life and spirit that it seems as if he could become almost anything, in time. But then, how passionate and willful he is! How often he makes my heart ache! Oh that God Himself would train and teach him!*" With these thoughts, which soon turned into prayers, she was so absorbed that she forgot to look after Lou until the bell began to ring for church. She then put on her bonnet and shawl, and went down to call him. When there was no answer, she went out to look for him, but he was nowhere to be found.

"*He's waiting in the study,*" she thought, and went there.

"Have you seen Lou?" she asked Papa.

"No, I thought he was with you. I'll call him."

He went out through the orchard and garden, and the winding paths under the trees, but no Lou was there.

"I can't find him," he said, coming back. "Abigail says she last saw him sitting in his carriage."

"Where can he be?" said Mama. "The bell is ringing, and here we are, waiting. Do you think anything happened to him? He *must* be somewhere about the grounds. I will look myself."

She went out, growing heartsick every moment. What if he had fallen down the well? Suppose some vagrant had lured him away?

Papa too, looked anxious. "It is just possible," he said, "that he has gone off to church alone. I'll go and see. I'll be back as soon as possible." The church was half a mile from the house, at the top of a steep hill. Service had begun, and the congregation was glad to see the tall, serious figure of Professor James, walking up the aisle to one of the pews near the pulpit where they normally sat.

But he instantly marched back again because no Lou was there.

Meanwhile Mama ran and looked down the well half a dozen times, and once more searched the orchard and the garden. Every moment she became more and more concerned, until at last she went up to her room, threw herself into a chair, and covered her face with her hands.

"O Lou! My little darling Lou! What has happened to you?" she cried aloud in her anguish. Instantly there came running out of a large closet, a little boy with a very red face and tangled hair. He threw himself into her arms, and burst out crying, as he covered her with kisses.

"Don't cry, dear Mama! Don't cry! Here I am, safe and sound!" he sobbed.

"Why Lou! Where have you been all this time? What were you doing in the closet? Didn't you hear us calling you?"

"I was hiding in the closet," said Lou, looking down.

"Hiding! For what?"

"I don't like to tell."

"But you must tell. I insist on knowing."

"I forgot."

"No, you didn't forget. You can't have forgotten so soon."

Lou was silent.

"Okay," said Mama, "since you will not obey me I'll have to punish you."

"I'll tell you then. I was going to hide in the closet until you and Papa had gone to church, and then I was going to come out and play."

Just then his papa came in to say that Lou was not at church, and was surprised to see him standing in front of his mama, and that she had a very angry look on her face.

"Listen to what this naughty little boy has been confessing," she said. "He heard us calling him, but was hiding all the time in my closet, hoping we would go to church without him, and that he could then come out and play."

"Okay," said Papa, "if he is likes the closet so much, he can go back and stay there. Cruel little boy! You have made mama quite ill with fright!"

"No, we have to give him the credit there," said his mama. "He came out the moment he saw that I was worried about him. But he has been guilty of something worse than the mere childish trick of hiding away. He has told me a lie. He said he forgot why he hid in the closet, because he was ashamed to admit the true reason."

"You must punish him severely for it," said his papa. "I will not have a liar in my house." Lou had never seen his father look so grieved and displeased.

Chapter 6

Near the close of this sad day, Lou's mama, who had been feeling very unwell, and not able to sit up, began to feel a little better. She had fled to God, her best Friend, just as the tired dove flew into the ark. She had told Him all Lou had done, and had asked Him to forgive him, and never to let him be so naughty again. And those who love God more than anybody else find a great deal of comfort in telling Him all about it when they are unhappy.

Lou was tired, too. He had cried a lot, partly because he was in disgrace, and partly because of the spanking he had gotten, and partly because he found his mama's closet a dark and lonely place when shut up in it as a punishment. Do you suppose his mama loved this naughty little boy? Yes, she loved him dearly.

She had suffered a great deal more pain in punishing him than he had in being punished. Every spank went across her heart, and left a mark there. But she knew that it was her duty to God to train this child to speak the truth and to be obedient.

Lou sat on a stool looking pale and unhappy. Under his eyes were two dark rings that showed how much he had cried, and his cheeks were quite pale.

He thought no one would ever love him again. "Come here, Lou," said Mama, and she held out her arms toward him. He came and climbed slowly and heavily into her lap.

"I'm sure you're sorry for all you have done today to make me sad and angry," she said.

"Yes, Mama." And his lip began to quiver again.

"Don't cry anymore. You have cried enough. You can be sorry now without crying. Do you think I love you, poor little boy?" Lou shook his head.

"I do love you; I love you more than I can tell. It's true that I've used my rod upon the same body that I've so often washed so tenderly; but as much as I love the little body that holds your soul, I love your soul better. Sometime your body will die, and be buried in the ground. But your soul will live forever; so I care most for that. I'm most anxious that it will be a soul that will be happy in heaven." While she was talking, she drew the tired little head close to her breast and with her soft hands caressed the pale face. Lou lay back in her arms, looking up into her eyes, devouring every word.

"You see," she went on, "Papa and I are going to live with God when we die. We love Him dearly, and we are glad we are going to live with Him. But we want you to go too. And God says 'no one who speaks falsely will stand in my presence.'[8] I've asked Him many times today to forgive you, and I think He has forgiven you. But you need to ask Him yourself, to be sure."

"I will," said Lou, in a soft voice. He felt truly sorry, and his heart was full of love for his dear mama. He wondered how she *could* love him, when he was so naughty. He prayed to God to forgive him, and to love him, and never to let him be so naughty again. He felt quite sure that he would be a perfectly good boy after this. He was now five years old and able to pray in words of his own, for whatever he chose; but he didn't want to have the trouble of trying very hard to do right. He wanted God to work a miracle, and make him good by force.

---

[8] He who works deceit shall not dwell within my house; He who tells lies shall not continue in my presence. Psalms 101:7

Chapter 7

Lou was now a tall, strong boy. He played outdoors in the cold winter weather all the time. His cousins, Jacob and Joshua, played with him in the snow. They sledded down hills, and made the air ring with their shouts of laughter. Sometimes they played the "Lost Traveler". Lou would lie down on the ground, and the others would cover him with snow, leaving a little hole for him to breathe through. Then Jacob would pretend to be one of the dogs of St. Bernard,[9] and would prowl around on all fours with his nose to the ground until suddenly, he would give a joyful bark, and Joshua would come running up, with a gray cloak folded around him to make him look like a monk. The two boys would then dig Lou out from the snow, give him a drink of milk from a bottle that hung around Jacob's neck, and rub his limbs to bring him to life. Then he was lifted to Jacob's back, and

---

[9] The name "St. Bernard" originates from the Great St. Bernard Hospice, a traveler's hospice on the often-treacherous St. Bernard Pass in the Western Alps between Switzerland and Italy. The pass, the lodge, and the dogs are named for Bernard of Menthon, the 11th century monk who established the station. "St. Bernard" wasn't in widespread use for dogs until the middle of the 19th century.-*Wikipedia*

trotted into the kitchen, where Abigail was often coaxed, not only to help rub the exhausted traveler, but to bring out good things for him to eat. That made the other boys eager to take their turn at getting lost in the snow.

One day Lou found a picture of some soldiers sitting by a campfire, boiling their kettle. He wished he wasn't a dunce and could read at that moment, for he wanted to know who the soldiers were and where they came from. But his papa and mama had gone off on a sleigh ride, and Abigail she said wouldn't read to him. She thought he ought to be ashamed of himself, not learning to read.

"My brother's little son Johnny," she said, "who's four or five months younger than you, can read quite nicely to his grandpa."

"Well, I'll catch up with him and get ahead of him. Of course, I'm going to learn to read sometime," said Lou.

"What are you fumbling around in my closet for? I've never seen such a boy. You're never still *one* minute. It's so nice to see a boy enjoying a book, and sitting down reading instead of tearing around as you do."

"I am not fumbling, and I am not tearing," said Lou. "I just want an old iron pot, that's all."

"What for?"

"Oh, to play with. I am going to get Jacob and Joshua, and we can play soldiers."

"Why does he want an iron pot to play soldiers with?" Abigail asked herself. "He'll leave it out in the snow, and get it all rusty; I know he will. And he's left the door open again with the weather as cold as Greenland's icy mountains." She shut the door with a quite a hard push.

Meanwhile Lou ran up to his uncle's to get his cousins. "I've thought of a great idea," he said. "Let's play that we're three soldiers that have been marching all day, and now we're tired and hungry. We'll pitch our tent, and make a fire, and boil our pot, and have dinner. Come on! I'll show you a picture of it."

"All right!" said the other boys. They all went racing down the street to the Lou's house, where they looked at the picture Lou showed them.

"What can we use for a tent?" asked Jacob.

"Oh, I know," cried Lou. "We can use Papa's shawl." He ran to get it, but now they had to figure out how to arrange it. None of them knew. Lou brought the rake, and the other boys found some beanpoles, but the tent looked very pitiful, as if the slightest breath of wind would blow it down.

"It doesn't matter how it looks," said Lou. "We are not going to live in it. We are going to make a fire, and boil our pot."

"A real fire?" asked Jacob.

"A real pot?" asked Joshua.

"Yes, a real fire and a real pot," said Lou. "You guys pick up some sticks and pile them up, and I'll get some more poles to hang the pot on." The boys obeyed. They gathered sticks from the floor of the woodhouse, and after a lot of trouble, they got three poles stuck in the snow, and hung their pot over the pile of sticks.

"Now I'll get a match and light the fire," said Lou.

"Will your mother let you?" asked Jacob.

"She isn't at home," said Lou. "But she wouldn't care, I know. She says she wants me to play outdoors all the time. So I have to have something to play with." He ran into the kitchen and there was no one there.

"Good," said Lou. "Now I can get a hot coal!" He grabbed the tongs and with them a large coal from the fire. The three boys then knelt down on the snow, and began to blow on the coal to make it kindle the sticks. They were soon all in a blaze.

"Now we need some water in our pot," said Lou. He stood thinking a moment. "If I go in again I might see Abigail, and she might ask what I want the water for. Then if she finds we've got a fire, I know just what she'll do. She'll take the tongs, and jerk one stick this way, and one stick that, and scold and scold. But there's no harm. Mama wouldn't care. Oh, I know what I'll do! I'll fill the pot with snow, and it will melt into water! I've often seen

Abigail melt snow. Yay! We're soldiers! We don't know where to get water; we'll use snow!"

The three boys, laughing and shouting, soon filled the pot. More wood was piled on, the snow melted, and the water began to warm.

"I think I'm hungry," said Lou. "We should cook our dinner now."

"I don't see anything to cook," said Jacob.

"Abigail will give us something," said Joshua.

"No she won't," said Lou. "I'll go down in the cellar and get some potatoes. Potatoes are good enough for soldiers." He ran in, leaving the door open, and was rushing through the kitchen when Abigail came down from the room above, where she had gone to change her dress.

"Now what is it?" she said.

"I want some potatoes to boil in my pot."

"Well, you can go down and get some. Shut the door after you."

"Okay," said Lou, and ran off, leaving the door open again. Abigail shut it after him.

"I guess I did the same thing when I was his age," she said. "But it is very aggravating."

The potatoes went into the pot very willingly. They didn't care whether they were boiled today or tomorrow, with skins on or off, for soldiers or for sailors. The little boys put on more wood and sat around watching their campfire.

"How soon will the potatoes be done?" asked Joshua. "I am very hungry."

"Yes, we're all hungry and tired," said Lou. "We've been marching all day. Our dinner will be ready soon; it only takes three minutes to boil potatoes."

"No, that's eggs," said Jacob.

"Potatoes aren't much bigger than eggs," said Lou. "I'll leave them in four minutes." While they watched their pot, and shivered with the cold, Abigail sat at her work by the kitchen fire. After a while she needed the tongs, but they were missing.

"Mercy on us!" she cried. "I do believe that child has taken my tongs! If he has, he's been making a fire! What should I do? I promised to look after him, and keep him out of mischief!"

She ran out not a moment too soon. A spark from the children's fire had caught a wisp of hay that was lying nearby. The hay had been blown along to some brushwood that was piled against the stable, and started a small fire. The stable itself, full of hay, would have caught next.

The surprised soldiers felt someone dash in among them and grab the tongs, and then saw Abigail scattering the brushwood with them, in all directions. They all started yelling, "Fire! Fire! Fire!" with all their might.

Just then Lou's papa and mama, driving into the yard, heard the cry and were quite startled.

Mama turned very pale, but she didn't have time to be frightened long. Papa jumped out of the sleigh, and pulled the wood apart, trampling it into the snow. Soon there was nothing left to tell tales but a smell of smoke, a camp kettle of boiling hot water, and three little guilty faces. Jacob and Joshua would have gladly run home, but they were so scared they couldn't move.

"Come into the house, all of you," said Lou's papa, "and tell us what's going on here. Mama, you'll have to take care of my hands for me; they are badly burned."

When they heard this, all three little soldiers began to cry.

Mama wrapped up the hands and when that was done, she asked questions until she found who was the ringleader.

"You don't need to cry, Jacob; nor you, Joshua," she said. "Lou is the one to blame. But I am most to blame for leaving him at home with nothing to do."

"I didn't mean to set the wood on fire," said Lou.

"Of course not. But you did set it on fire, and in a few more moments the stable would have caught, and then the woodhouse, and then the house itself. We would have lost our pleasant home, our pictures, our books, our clothes; everything we have."

Lou looked very sad.

"I'll never do that again," he said.

"No, I don't think you will. But you may get into some other trouble. I'm definitely going to start teaching you to read. Then when I'm gone, you can entertain yourself without setting the house on fire."

Chapter 8

THE VERY NEXT day, Lou's reading lessons began. He learned very easily. When he was pleasant and patient, it was fun to teach him. His mama was surprised to see how fast he caught on. But, on the other hand, she was surprised to see how he *hated* to have the time come for his lessons. She, who knew the comfort and pleasure of being able to read to herself, wondered why Lou was not more eager to enjoy it too. But learning to read is always a chore.

"Mama," said Lou, "I'll tell you what will be a good way. The days I'm good, and don't complain about my lessons, you could promise to read me a story about a good boy. And the days I do complain, you could read me a story about a bad boy."

"Sure, that would be a fine way," said Mama, laughing. "Since you prefer hearing about bad boys, I would be giving you more fun on your naughty days. But I think it would be better for you to be good all the time."

"But I can't, Mama. You see I can't. I want to be good, but something in me makes me naughty.

Why don't God make everybody good? He *can*, so why don't He?"

"I don't know. I don't expect, ignorant as I am, to understand everything done by such a wise and wonderful Being as God."

"Oh Mama! You're not ignorant! You know everything!"

His mama smiled.

"Never mind," she said, "We're talking about things you don't understand."

"Well, Mama, I want to know one thing. Can God do anything he chooses?"

"Certainly."

Lou looked doubtful.

"Can He, Papa?" he asked.

"Yes, of course," said Papa, surprised at such a question.

"Well, can He make a stone so large and heavy that he can't lift it Himself?"

Papa looked at Mama and Mama looked at Papa.

"Lou," said Papa at last, "it says in the Bible that the secret of the Lord is with them that fear Him.[10] That means that those who love Him don't ask such questions as you have just asked. They know what He can do by their love for Him. They

---

[10] The secret of the LORD [is] with those who fear Him, And He will show them His covenant. Psalms 25:14

are not eager to think of something He can't do; they rejoice to think He can do all things. Yes, and I rejoice to think that out of this ignorant little boy of mine, He can make a wise, good man."

Lou didn't quite understand what his papa had been saying, but he felt a little less arrogant at the end of the talk than he did at the beginning. He walked off quietly, instead of running and shouting, as he usually did when study hour was over.

"*What should I do, now?*" he thought. "*I wish I had a brother the same age as me. Then I would always have somebody to play with me. Jacob has Joshua, and Joshua has Jacob, and I don't see why I don't have somebody.*" He opened the front door, and saw a boy running eagerly along on the sidewalk.

"Hello, Lou James! Don't you want to go and see a great fat ox?"

"Yes, yes, where is it?"

"Just past the tavern. Come on! It weighs four thousand paounds." Lou darted into the house, his eyes shining, and about twice as big as usual.

"May I go and see a great fat ox that weighs four thousand paounds?" he cried.

"What, alone?"

"No, with another boy."

"What boy is it?"

"Mr. Jefferd's boy."

"Oh no, I can't have you go with that boy. He uses very bad language, I've been told. I don't think he's a good boy, at all."

"I'll run out and ask him if he is a good boy!" said Lou, eagerly.

"No, no, that won't do. Of course he'll say he is. I wouldn't think you would want to go and see a fat ox. I wouldn't."

"That's because you're not a little boy, that hasn't got any brother," said Lou. "It is a great big ox and weighs four thousand paounds."

"Don't say *paounds*," insisted Mama.

"I'll take you myself, Lou," said his papa. "I don't think you will enjoy it that much, but I'll go with you. As for that Jefferds boy, I want you to keep out of his way. He says bad words." They started off down the street.

"What are bad words?" asked Lou.

"I don't think I can explain what they are, to such a little boy as you."

"Couldn't you say a bad word, just one, for me to hear, Papa?"

"No, I couldn't. You'll hear bad language soon enough without my help. I hope you never will use it yourself."

"Is *ox* a bad word?"

"No, of course not."

"Is *paounds* a bad word?"

"No, it's just pronounced wrong. It should be *pounds*. Just be content with keeping out of bad company, and you won't hear bad words."

They came now to a large tent in which the ox was kept. A crowd of men and boys stood idling outside, laughing and talking. The ox had its horns decorated with red, white, and blue ribbon, and was a huge, awkward creature. Lou didn't find the sight of it as delightful as he had expected.

"Let's go, Papa," he said. "It isn't nice here at all."

"I am glad I let you come," said his papa, as they pushed their way out into the open air. "You're satisfied now, and never will want to see such a sight again."

"No, Papa. I never will. I thought it would be a lot bigger. Maybe as big as our house."

"In that case I would have been curious to see it myself. But these days, no animals exist who are that enormous."

"Were there, in old times?"

Yes, the bones of animals have been found and put together, that must have belonged to creatures that were really immense."

"Did you ever see one?"

"Which, the animals, or the bones?"

"The bones."

"Yes, I saw one in the British Museum. We are having a model made of it, to put in our college museum."

"A model?" asked Lou.

"Yes. That's something made to look exactly like the bones in the British Museum."

"Will I get to see it?"

"Of course."

Chapter 9

"Oh man, I'm so tired!" said Lou, yawning, with his hands over his head. "The sermon was *so* long!"

"Yes, it was long," said his papa, "and you sat very still. I'll tell you a Bible story, to relax you."

"Oh, I know every single Bible story now," said Lou. "Every single one."

"Have you ever heard the story of Job?"

"No, Papa. That isn't a story. I've heard some of it read."

"We'll see," said Papa. "Who was Job?"

"Job? Job was a—he was a—he was a man; or else he was a woman."

"What happened to him?"

"Well—he—well, I don't think I know."

"No, I see you don't. Okay. Once upon a time it happened that Satan was in heaven—"

"Satan! How did *he* get into heaven?" asked Lou, surprised.

"I don't know. I only know he was there."

"Maybe he flied up. Flew, I mean. But how did he get the door open?"

"The Bible doesn't tell. He was there, and God asked him if he knew Job."

"What made God ask that?"

"Well, Satan said he had been going back and forth on the earth, and walking up and down on it. And then God asked him if he had seen Job, and knew what a good man he was."

"What did Satan say?"

"He didn't say whether he had seen Job, or not. Satan is not the kind to give a straight answer to a question. He only said that if Job was a good man, as God said he was, it was because he had everything he wanted. Do you think it would make *you* good, to have everything you wanted?"

"Sure, Papa. Then I wouldn't have anything to whine about. Now if I had a little brother, I would always have somebody to play with me, and so I wouldn't be bugging you and Mama."

"Would you never quarrel with your little brother? Suppose you had one, and he slept with you in your bed and took almost all the room; what would you do?"

"I guess I would push him a little," said Lou, who remembered the night he slept with one of his cousins.

"And then he would push you back, and you would both become angry. Having a brother wouldn't make you good. Satan knew he wasn't speaking the truth when he said that about Job. God knew it too, and so he told Satan he could take away all Job's things, and see how he would act then."

"Did Job have many things?"

"Yes. He had seven sons, and three daughters. And he had seven thousand sheep, and three thousand camels, and five hundred yoke of oxen, and five hundred donkeys."

"What a lot of salt it must have taken to salt so many sheep!" said Lou. "And Job must have had a lot of workers to take care of so many animals. I wish I could have seen all those sheep and camels and oxen and donkeys!"

"Yes, that many sheep would eat a lot of salt. And Job did have many workers to take care of his animals. He was the richest man in that country. And his sons must have been rich too, because each of them had a house of his own. They took turns having their sisters come to have parties with them."

"That made seven parties," said Lou. "I wish I had been there!"

"Yes. One day it was the turn of the eldest brother to have the party at his house. And while they were all eating and drinking together, a messenger came to Job and said that some men had taken away all his oxen and all his donkeys, and killed all the men who were taking care of them! And then another came saying that fire had fallen from heaven and burned up all the sheep, and all the men who took care of them, and that he only was left alive to tell the news! And then another came, who said that three bands of robbers had stolen all the camels, and only left one man alive. While he was speaking, yet a fourth man came and said that while all Job's ten children were feasting together, a wind had come from the wilderness and blown down the house they were in, and killed everybody in it, except himself."

"Oh, no!" cried Lou. "Poor Job! That's terrible! What did he do?"

"He fell down on the ground, and worshipped God. He said he had nothing when he came into the world, and now he had nothing to carry out of it. And he said that the Lord had given him everything he had, and the Lord had taken it away, and ended with, 'Blessed be the name of the Lord!'"

Chapter 10

I T WAS NOW time for dinner, and after dinner Papa read aloud to Mama. Lou listened a little while, but he didn't understand a word. *"How can Mama like to hear such books?"* he thought. *"The house is full of storybooks, and yet Mama likes to hear Papa read things that sound just like sermons."* He walked to the window. It was an October day, and a single fly was buzzing on the windowpane. He felt as lonely as Lou did.

"I wish I had something to do," the fly thought. *"If I could get outside, I could play, but this window is shut all the time now. I'm hungry, too. I think I'll go and buzz in that little boy's face."* So the fly settled on Lou's forehead, and Lou felt a little fine, sharp pain when the fly bit him.

"Go away, old fly," he said, shaking his head. But the fly only moved a little way, and made another fine, sharp pain on his forehead. Lou shook his head again, but the fly didn't move. "Mama, this fly is bothering me. He keeps biting and biting, and I keep shaking and shaking, and he doesn't fall off!"

"Yes, and the world keeps spinning round and round, and none of us fall off," said Mama.

"Hey, Mama! Aren't we inside of the world?"

"No, we're on the outside. But don't talk now. I want to listen to Papa read."

"On the outside!" repeated Lou to himself. "I don't believe it. The world is round, Papa says so. If it keeps spinning and spinning, and if everybody was on the outside, they'd fall off unless they held on to each other."

"Mama! May I have an apple?"

"Yes, but don't talk." Lou ran down for an apple.

"Now I have to get it spinning and get the fly to land on it," he said. He thought a long time what to do. At last he tied a string to the stem of the apple, and twisted the string, and then let it untwist slowly. "Ha! That's the good of the Rollo books!" he said. "I learned that in a Rollo book.[11] Now to get the fly on. Come here, old fly." The fly, however, was buzzing on the window and paid no attention to Lou. Lou held the apple near it but the fly flew off.

"You silly old thing! I wasn't going to hurt you! Oh, if you'd only land on my apple a minute, I'd give you a piece of it. This apple is the round world, old fly, and you're one of the residents."

"What are you doing, Lou?" asked his mama. "I didn't give you the apple for a toy, but to eat. Come, let me brush your hair, and get you ready for church."

"Is it time for church?" asked Lou, greatly surprised. "It's only a minute or two since dinner! Papa, will you tell me some more about Job after church? I like Job."

"Yes, I will tell you more, if you're as quiet in church this afternoon, as you were this morning."

"I saw that Jefferds boy at church this morning, and he wrestled all the time."

"Wrestled? Wrestled with whom?"

"With himself."

"What can the child mean?" asked Papa.

---

[11] Rollo is the main character in a series of Books for children by Jacob Abbot.

"Maybe he means that he was restless," said Mama.

"Yes, that's it. That's what I mean."

Chapter 11

"Now Papa, I'm ready to listen," said Lou.

"Remember that after Job had lost all he had, he blessed God? What if I went up to your room, and took down all your pictures, grabbed all your books, toys, pencils and paper, your box of paints, your kitten, everything your Mama and I have given you. If you ran and threw your arms around me, and said 'Dear Papa! Everything I had was given to me by you and Mama. And I love you just as much as I did before, even though you took all my things.' That would be like Job, when God allowed all he had to be taken away."

Lou's heart swelled. "Do you think you will ever do that, Papa?" he asked anxiously.

"No, I don't think so. Now, to go on with my story. Satan appeared before God once more, and God asked the same question about Job that He had asked the first time. And Satan gave another crooked answer. He wouldn't admit that Job had been patient, and his love for God hadn't changed in his time of trouble. He only said that as long as Job felt well and strong, it was easy to be good, but that if God would make him sick, he would curse him to his face. Then God told Satan he could make Job as sick as he wanted. So Satan covered him with boils, from his feet to his head."

"What are boils?"

"They are very painful sores. Even one will make a grown man grouchy and miserable. Think how bad it must be to be covered with them from head to foot!"

"Was Job grouchy?"

"Wait and see. When Job's wife saw the miserable state he was in, she thought the best thing that could happen to him, would be to die. He had no children to love, his riches were all gone, and now he was in terrible pain. She said to him something like this. 'Are you going to love God in spite of the way he has treated you? You should curse Him and die.' And Job answered, 'You speak like a foolish woman. Should we receive good from God, and not bad?' You see he loved God so much that even in his suffering, he couldn't bear to listen to people speaking badly about Him.

Now Job had three friends. Their names were Eliphaz, Bildad, and Zophar. When they heard what had happened to him, they came to tell him how sorry they were for him and to mourn with him. As they came near him, he was so changed that at first they didn't know it was him. Then when they saw that it really was him, sitting in the ashes, they couldn't help crying. Every one of them tore his robe, and sprinkled dust on his head."

"What did they do that for?"

"It was the custom of the people in that country to do that when they were in trouble. Then they sat down on the ground with him for seven days and seven nights, without saying a word, because his grief was so great."

"Seven days and seven nights! That's a whole week!" cried Lou.

"Finally, Job began to speak. He said he was suffering so terribly that it would have been better for him to have died the day he was born, and that every dreadful thing he had feared, had come upon him.

"Then his friend Eliphaz, instead of telling Job how sorry he was for him, began to find fault with him. He said that Job had often urged people in trouble to bear it patiently, and now was giving up himself. And he said it was a good thing to be disciplined by God. Now this is true, but when a man is in such misery as Job was, he can't listen to such things. All he wants is to have somebody take his hand, and say 'Oh, how sorry I am for you!'

Suppose you fell down and broke your leg, and instead of picking you up and kissing you and running for the doctor, I said, 'Well, you like to hear stories about boys who are heroic and are brave when they are hurt. I'm surprised you cry so much! Besides, it's a lucky thing that you've broken your leg. Maybe it will help you stop doing bad things!'"

"What did Job say to Eliphaz?"

"He said he wished all his sufferings could be weighed, so that his friends could see how heavy they were. He said they would weigh as much as the sand on the shore.

"And he said he couldn't sleep because he was so sad, or keep still because he was in such pain. And that in the morning he wished it was night, and at night he wished it was morning. Then Bildad began to speak. He said that maybe the reason why God had destroyed all Job's children was because they were wicked. And that if Job were as good as he ought to be, God wouldn't cause him to have so much trouble. Job answered that he knew that God was a just God, and that he wished he knew how he had displeased him, and could have a little rest from his pain before he died.

"Then Zophar accused him of talking too much, and said he had better think over all his sins and repent of them. Job was very sad at the way his friends talked. He said they should learn wisdom from the beasts of the field, and the fowls of the air. He knew that he loved and trusted God, and that he was willing to know if his sins had caused his problems, and he said so.

"Then Eliphaz reproved Job again, and said he didn't fear God or pray as much as he should."

"Poor Job!" said Lou's mama, looking up from her book. "I never pitied him half enough.

How little those men, in good health and with no sorrows of their own, knew how to pity him!"

"Yes, Job finally said, 'you are all miserable comforters!' And he tried to make them see how he was suffering. But Bildad told him he ought to be more patient. And Eliphaz said that when he was a rich man, he had not fed the hungry, and had sent beggars away empty, and that this was the reason why God had punished him. Job answered that this was not true. He had given to all the poor he knew, and had even searched for those he didn't know. He said he had made the widow's heart to sing for joy, and had been eyes to the blind and feet to the lame.

"Now Job had another friend named Elihu. He had not dared to speak all this time because he was the youngest, but now he began and made a long speech, in which he found fault with Job and with all his friends. And then they heard God's voice speaking to Job out of a whirlwind. And he told Eliphaz, Bildad, and Zophar that he was angry with them for what they had been saying, and that they must take seven bulls, and seven rams, and go to Job and offer up for themselves a burnt offering, and then Job would pray for them. So the three friends did that. While poor, afflicted Job was praying for his friends, God healed his boils, and gave him twice as many riches as he had before. And all his brothers and sisters and everybody that used to know him, came to eat with him in his new house, and they all tried to comfort him for all the trouble the Lord had brought upon him. And every man gave him a piece of money, and a gold earring."

"Hey!" said Lou. "What did Job want with earrings?"

His papa smiled. "People liked to own lots of that kind of jewelry in those days. Maybe Job wore earrings himself. Job had fourteen thousand sheep now, and six thousand camels, and a thousand yoke of oxen, and a thousand donkeys. And God gave him seven sons, and three daughters who were the most beautiful of all the young women in the land. Job lived one hundred and forty years after this, and didn't die until he was a very old man."

"Thank you, Papa," said Lou. "I will never forget this story. I'm going to try to be as patient as Job was; then God will love me."

"God loves you even if you aren't as patient as Job," said Papa smiling.

Chapter 12

"Take a basket and come with me, Lou," said his mama. "I'm going to buy some things which you can bring home." Lou ran quickly for the basket, and followed her down the street.

"I am so glad we're going, Mama," he said, "because Mr. Mason often gives me things when I go to his shop with you. What do you want to buy? Things to eat or things to wear?"

"I am going to buy ribbon, for one thing. And some salt, for another. And I am out of needles, too."

Mr. Mason stood behind the counter, looking very cheerful. He had almost everything to sell. In big cities there are no shops like this. In the country, where there are only a very few shops, all sorts of things are mixed together: sugar and flour and butter, pails and tubs, rakes and hoes, calico and wool and flannel, pills and castor-oil, needles and thread, and shoes and boots.

"I need a pair of shoes for my little boy," said Lou's mama. "And do you have any green ribbon? We need some sugar, too. Oh, and I want some needles. Do you have any that you can recommend?"

"I'm out of needles," said Mr. Mason. "My last order came in entirely ruined. They got wet somehow." He took down a box full of papers of needles, and showed her how rusty they were.

"Are they all spoiled?" asked Lou. "That's too bad!"

"Yes, they're good for nothing," said Mr. Mason. "I give them to my little girls now and then, when they pretend they own a shop."

"Oh, that must be fun!" said Lou. "I never played that."

"Then here is a box of needles for you," said Mr. Mason. "That is, if your mama doesn't mind."

Mama said it was okay, and she went on looking at the things she wanted to buy.

"I'll take the whole roll of that ribbon," she said.

"My basket is getting full," said Lou. "It's a good thing I'm so strong. May I wear my new shoes home, and carry the old ones?"

"Yes, you may. Come on, I'm ready now."

When they got home, Abigail took all the things from the basket that belonged in the kitchen, and Lou went up to his mama's room with her, carrying the rest.

"Mama, isn't the ribbon you bought rolled on a little round block?" he asked.

"I guess it is. Why, do you want it?"

"Yes, I am going to make a little clock with it."

"Okay."

She unrolled the ribbon, and gave him the block. Lou ran for his pencils and paper, and a pair of round-pointed scissors that he was allowed to cut with. He laid the block on the paper and drew a line all around it to make a circle. Then he cut it out and it was just the size of the block.

"Now Mama, this is the face of my clock. Will you make the numbers on it?"

"What numbers?" asked Mama, who was measuring her ribbon, and not paying much attention to him.

"All the numbers. 1, 2, and so on."

"Oh, I see, okay. Well, what next?"

"Now may I use a little glue to stick it on?"

"Yes, but don't spill it, and don't get it all over your numbers."

"I'll be very careful." He pasted on the paper very neatly. Then he tried to think what he would do for hands. At last he cut them, one long and one short, from a piece of thick paper. Next he nailed them to the middle of his clock with a very small tack. But when that was done he couldn't move them.

"*That* won't do," he said. "The hands of a real clock move. I drove the tack in too tight." He worked away at it a long time, trying to loosen the tack. His mama glanced at him now and then, glad to see his perseverance. At last he came joyfully toward her.

"Look at my little clock, Mama!" he cried. "Please tell me what time it is, so that I can set it."

"It's twenty minutes past eleven. Wow, can you really move the hands? Your clock is quite an ingenious invention."

"Yes, and I can hang it up. Look, Mama. It has a little loop to hang it by. It is good that you made me learn how to tell time! I couldn't have made this nice little clock, if you hadn't."

"Yes, and it's good that I make you learn to read, since you won't learn on your own."

"Yes, you dear Mama, it is. Can I read to you now?"

"Yes, I'm not busy now."

Lou ran to get his book. He could read very well, in short words. His mama said he had learned by magic almost, he had improved so fast.

Chapter 13

In the afternoon Lou remembered his box of needles, and that he had meant to play shopkeeper.

"Mama," he said, "will you lend me some of your things to play with? Things that men keep in a shop?"

"I will, if you will take good care of them, and bring them back to me in perfect order."

She gave him all the new spools of thread she had bought that morning, some pieces of tape, a paper of pins, and a pair of scissors. Then she told him where he could find some bars of soap, some little boxes, and several small bottles.

"But first, Lou, you need a shop," she said, "with places for hanging things, and a counter. But since you don't have one, I'll have to help you make one."

"Do you have time, Mama?"

"Oh, it won't take long. You can go up to the attic to find a box. An old wood soapbox will do, and if you see any smaller boxes lying around, you may bring them."

Lou hurried off, his cheeks rosy with happiness. "*I guess I'll have a nice shop,*" he thought. In the attic he found a small cabinet that had once been used for minerals. It was full of little shelves, rising one above another. But it was too big. He couldn't lift it. He tried first one end, then the other, but no, it wouldn't move. Just then, two little heads appeared, coming up the attic stairs.

"Jacob, is that you?" cried Lou. "Come right here and help me move this box. It's as heavy as lead. You help too, Joshua." The three little fellows pushed, and lifted, and coaxed. The box moved just a tiny bit, then started off with a jerk to the edge of the stairs.

"Hurray! Here it goes!" cried Lou, and sure enough, away went the box down the stairs, making a loud noise on the way. His mama thought that the three boys must have fallen and broken their necks. She came running to the foot of the stairs, where she found them very frightened at the noise they had made.

"Oh, that old cabinet," she said. "How could you three little things even move it? Well, since it is here, and not quite broken to pieces, I'll let you use it for a shop. You can keep some things on the shelves, and some in the drawers. But then I will want you to keep it in good order."

"Yes, Aunty."

"Yes, Mama."

Lou knew Mama would be too weak to help move the cabinet. "Can I ask Abigail to come and help us lift it up, and put it somewhere?" asked Lou.

"Yes, you may keep it in your own room. But don't tumble anything else down the stairs, and frighten me again. If you do, I'll stop growing!" The boys laughed.

"Don't you think you're about big enough as you are, Mama?" asked Lou. "I wouldn't think you would want to grow anymore."

"Except in goodness," said Mama. "I'd like to grow in goodness until I become quite perfect. And so would you, little boys."

Abigail came now to help get the old cabinet into Lou's room, and very soon the six busy hands had covered the shelves and filled the drawers. Besides what his mama had lent him, Lou had a lot of things from the kitchen. Abigail gave him some cloves, a few nutmegs, some salt, a little sugar, and some coffee and tea. She filled his little bottles with liquids of different colors, and he thought he had various medicines for sale, when he really had cold coffee in one vial, and cold tea in another, and in a third some of the water in which she had put indigo, for the clothes she had been washing.

"Oh, thank you, Abigail!" cried Lou. "Now when you're sick, all you'll have to do is come to my shop and I'll give you a dose of medicine that will cure you right away."

"I hope I won't be sick," said Abigail. "But if I am, I certainly will come to you unless you charge too high a price."

The little shop that cost nobody any money, and almost no trouble, was a lot of fun for the three boys for a long time. Lou's mama had to buy things from it very often. Whenever she wanted a pin, or a spool of thread, or some tape, she bought it there. She usually paid for it with round pieces of paper, cut to look like money. But now and then she paid for what she bought with apples or gingerbread or candy or a bit of maple sugar. Abigail bought some of the rusty needles and rubbed them with sandpaper, and used them to truss the chickens and turkeys when they were ready to roast.

Chapter 14

"Come here, Lou," said his mama one morning when the mail had just come in. "I have something so funny to show you!" Lou threw down the hammer that he had been playing with and ran to the table where she sat. "Look at this little card," said his mama. "A little baby has just sent it to me in the mail."

"What for? How could it? What's its name? Where does it live?"

"What a string of questions! He sent me his card to let me know of his arrival in this world. I suppose he got his papa to have the cards printed. His name is Walter Fisk, Jr. and he lives in New York."

"Did I send my card to anybody when I first arrived?"

"No, I don't think you ever heard of such a thing. I am sure I never did. I think it is a very pretty, funny little card. And I am very glad that there is a little Walter Fisk, Jr. in the world, because he is making his papa and mama so glad."

"Do you suppose they are as glad as you and papa were, when I came?"

"Oh, I don't know. It doesn't seem to me that anybody could be half as glad as we were. If you little darlings only knew how dearly your papas and mamas love you, I don't see how you could ever be naughty. And if we grown up people only knew how much God loves us, *we* would always be good, too."

"Mama," said Lou, after a little silence, "does Papa ever read anything but the Bible? Whenever I go into the study, he's always reading it. And there are lots and lots of books in the study."

"Of course he reads other books. But he reads and studies the Bible most of all. I hear carriage wheels. Run to the window, and see who's coming."

"It's a lady and a little boy," said Lou. "The boy is just as big as I am. I'm so glad! Now I have someone to play with." Abigail let the lady in and she entered the room. Lou's mama went to meet her, and then spoke to the little boy, who didn't answer but looked up into her face with a smile that showed he had heard what she said.

"Will you come and play with me, little boy?" asked Lou. The little boy smiled again, and rose and followed Lou into the garden. As soon as he had gone, his mama began to talk about old school days when she and Lou's mama used to be good friends.

"You haven't changed much, Laura," she said. "You look as young as ever. And what a fine little boy you have! As for me, I've had so much trouble that I've grown old fast. You have heard about my Julius, haven't you?"

"No, nothing bad of him that I remember."

"Just think, he is five years old and has never spoken a word!"

"Poor little guy!" said Lou's mama. "Has he lost his hearing?

"No, he hears as well as you or I. And I'm sure he could talk also, if he wanted to. We've tried everything to make him talk, but he won't. He makes signs for everything."

"How very strange! What if you don't pay any attention to his signs; wouldn't that get him to speak?"

"No, we've tried that, many times. I want you to see him. Which way has he gone?"

"He is just outside; should I tell Lou to bring him in?"

"No, I'll call him. Then you'll see that he can hear just as well as other children." She stepped to the window and said, "Come in now, Julius. I want Mrs. James to see you." Julius came instantly, followed by Lou, who whispered to his mama, "He won't talk to me. He only smiles and nods his head and moves his hands."

"Julius," said Mrs. James in a kind voice, "I'm very glad to see you. How do you like being in the country?"

Julius smiled and looked pleasantly in her face. Then he opened his left hand and made motions with the other as if he were spreading bread and butter.

"He's hungry," said Lou. "He wants some bread and butter."

"Yes, that's his way of asking for it. Oh Julius! How can you upset me like this?" said his mama.

"He doesn't know how much you love him," said Lou. "If he did he would never be naughty. But he hasn't been naughty since he came here," he added earnestly.

"Don't you think it's naughty not to use the tongue God has given him to talk with, and to make signs instead?"

"Oh, does he have a tongue?" cried Lou in great surprise. "I thought he didn't have one. And I asked God to give him a tongue."

"You dear child!" said the lady, kissing him. "Just think! My poor little boy has never prayed to God in his life."

"Maybe he has in his heart," said Lou's mama. "Take him out to Abigail, Lou my dear, and give him whatever he wants."

"It is very strange," she added, as the children left the room together. "Has he been with other children much?"

"No, not much. His little sister died a year ago, and I've kept him with me, most of the time. He behaved very strangely at the time of her death. He used to go out with a bow and arrow and aim at the sky, and when we asked what that meant, he made signs that he was going to shoot God because He had taken away his little sister."

"It's amazing that he could make you understand that just by signs! He is smart enough, then."

"Oh, yes, he is. And now what would you advise me to do with him?"

"I don't know. Where are you staying?"

"At the hotel. I have rooms there for a few weeks."

"Then how about leaving Julius with us. We're not used to his signs, and he may find that he has to talk to be understood."

"I'm afraid he'll cry when he misses me. But you're very kind. I think I will leave him. Tell him I'll come for him as soon as he asks for me. And I'm sure I don't need to ask you to hold and comfort him a little, when he cries for me."

Lou's mama promised. She felt quite sure that if anything could open the mouth of a silent child, it would be the loss of his mother.

After a while Julius and Lou came in, and the face of Julius said clearly, "Where is my mother?" Lou's mama drew him to her and kissed him.

"Your mama will come just as soon as you call for her. Try, dear. Try to say, 'Come Mama!'" But Julius was silent, and his eyes filled with tears. He went and sat in a corner, looking sad and sorrowful. Lou and his mama did everything that they could think of to cheer him up, but he ignored them. At last, night came. It was bedtime and no dear mama was there. He watched the door whenever it opened, but she didn't come. He wouldn't go to bed or eat. Lou's mama began to wish she had not decided to keep him.

"It's a cruel test," she said at last. "I'm sure the child *cannot* speak. I must take him to his mama." Julius stopped crying and listened. He had always been told that he could speak if he chose, and the idea that he could not was new to him.

"Oh!" he cried, "can't I speak?" Then there was great laughing and crying for joy. Professor James and Mrs. James hurried to take the little boy to the hotel, and there they saw his mama learn the joy of folding her child in her arms, and hearing him say "I love you, Mama!" Lou was already in bed when all this happened, but when his mama told him about it the next day, he said it was all because he had prayed for Julius. His mama thought so too!

Julius talked after this, but not like other children. He left out every word that he could show by a sign. This story seems almost too strange to be true, but it really is true!

Part 4

Chapter 1

It was a cold November morning. The air was quite cold, and it pinched Lou's cheeks until it made them rosy. He was sliding on a narrow strip of thin ice in the garden and having a very fun time. His mama had not come down to breakfast, and his papa had gone to college prayers.

"*I wish this ice slide were a mile long,*" thought Lou. And just as he thought that, his foot slipped and he fell flat on his back. He was not hurt much, but he was bruised a little.

"I'm not going to cry for that," he said, picking himself up. "I'm as patient as Job." He ran to take another slide, and this time he fell flat on his face. The next minute he let out a loud scream, and got up and ran toward the house. As he ran, he felt the blood running from his upper lip and his nose. He forgot all about Job, and cried harder than ever. Abigail came running out of the kitchen.

"What's the matter now?" she called. "Don't scream like that! You'll scare your mama to death." But Lou hopped up and down on the kitchen floor, and held both hands to his face. Abigail pulled them away and filled a bowl with water, and washed away the blood.

"You couldn't cry louder if your neck was broken," she said.

"I couldn't cry at all if my neck was broken," said Lou, stopping in the midst of his shrieks. "Don't you know that?" After saying this, Lou took up his cry just where he left off, and made such a noise that his mama heard him and came running downstairs. By this time his nose and upper lip were so swollen that they felt very odd.

"I fell down on the ice and hurt myself really bad," he said when he saw his mama.

"Yes," she said, "I'm sorry that happened. I hope you haven't knocked out any of your teeth. Let me see! No, your teeth are all safe. Come and have your breakfast." Lou followed her, sobbing, to the dining room. She poured his bowl of cereal and milk. He began to eat, but his lip was so swollen, that he could hardly get the spoon into his mouth.

"Mama, maybe it will make me better," he said in a trembling voice.

"What? The cereal and milk?"

"No, getting hurt. I mean gooder; it may make me gooder."

"Well, maybe it will. But how?"

"Oh, it will punish me for all the naughty things I've done." He was greatly sobered by his fall, and instead of rushing out after breakfast, he hung around his mother, watching all she did. First she washed the silver and rubbed it dry. Then she washed the cups and saucers and plates, and put everything neatly away. Then Abigail came and took the remaining dishes from the table, shook the tablecloth, folded it, and put it away. Many little birds that lived nearby came hopping up to the doorsteps where Abigail had shaken the tablecloth. They came every morning to pick up the crumbs that she scattered around.

"What are you going to do now, Mama?" asked Lou, following her.

"We've had our breakfast, and the birds have had theirs," she replied, "and now my plants want theirs."

"Their breakfast?" repeated Lou. "Plants can't eat."

"No, but they can drink. A lady once told me that she sent a plant home by sea that had been given to her when she was on a trip."

"How could she send it by sea?"

"On a ship, of course."

"Oh, I get it."

"And she was afraid it would die without any water on the way. So she fastened a piece of paper on it that said, '*Please give me a drink!*'"

Lou began to laugh, but his lip felt so puffy and weird that he had to stop. Meanwhile, his mama gave each plant some water. She picked off all the dead leaves, and brushed the dust from the good ones. This took a long time, because she had lots of plants.

Chapter 2

"And now what are you going to do, Mama?" asked Lou.

"I am going to neaten up the study."

"Why doesn't Abigail do that?"

"Abigail has other things to do. She has beds to make, clothes to wash and food to cook."

"But that doesn't take all the time. She often sits and reads or sews."

"I would hope so, my dear. She needs rest as much as you or I."

"But Mama, don't you want to be a lady, like Mrs. Nelson. She doesn't wash the breakfast dishes or dust the furniture or do any work."

Mama laughed. "I *am* a lady, even so," she said. "And I can neaten the study for that very reason. See, I know just how to arrange the books to make them look nice on Papa's table. I know which ones to leave out, and which ones to put on the shelves. Papa likes to have me take care of his papers, too."

"You never get any time to play, you poor Mama. I wish we were richer, and could hire two Abigails."

"We are rich enough. We have everything we need, and more too. Don't you know that in the Bible there is this verse—'Give me neither poverty nor riches?'[12] Your papa and I never had to say that. God gave us neither poverty nor riches, without our asking." By this time the study was in order, and Mama was free to do whatever she wanted. "Now it's my playtime," she said. "I'm going to draw. If you don't feel like going out to slide anymore, you may bring your pencils and your drawing book and sit with me at the table."

"I don't want to slide. I feel too tired all over," said Lou. His two falls had jarred and bruised him a lot, so he went to get his drawing book. His mama had given him several lessons, and he was learning to make straight lines. But normally he was so full of energy that he didn't like to be called in to draw.

"It's good that I fell down and hurt myself," he said, as he sat by his mama's side, busily at work. "It makes me like to draw." They were very happy, sitting side by side.

"Sometimes I almost wish you were a little girl, Lou," said Mama, when they had been silent a

---

[12] Remove falsehood and lies far from me; Give me neither poverty nor riches—Feed me with the food allotted to me; lest I be full and deny You, And say, "Who is the LORD?" Or lest I be poor and steal, and profane the name of my God. Proverbs 30:8-9

long time. "It's so lovely having you sit so quietly here with me. If you were a little girl, you would probably want to do just what I do. You would like to work and draw and paint and read, and what nice times we would have together! As it is, if you feel well and the weather is not too stormy, you want to be outside all the time. If I didn't make you do it, you would never touch a book or a pencil."

"But you say you like to have me stay outside so I'll be strong and healthy," said Lou.

"That's true. And even if you *were* a little girl, I wouldn't want you always cooped up in the house."

By this time Lou was tired of drawing.

"Mama," he said, "do you feel sorry for me because I'm hurt?"

Mama looked at his swollen lip, which seemed to be growing larger every minute, and replied, "Yes, I feel very sorry for you."

"Do you feel sorry enough to tell me a story?" His mama laughed.

"I suppose I do," she said. "But I've told you all the stories I know, over and over. I guess I can come up with one more."

Chapter 3

In a barnyard, once upon a time,
There lived two hens, who talked in rhyme.
The one was white, with chickens ten;
The other was a turkey hen.
Each with her brood went to and fro,
Teaching the young ones how to go.
The white hen to her children said,

"Your legs, I'm thankful, are not red.
Look at those turkeys! I declare,
They every one with heads go bare!
They wear their throats without a feather,

They all will die of croup together.
Or if the sun would shine too hot,
They'd all be sun struck on the spot.
And then the noise the creatures make!
Do plug your ears, for pity's sake!"
The turkey hen this language heard,
And greatly was her anger stirred.
The comb she wore upon her head
Turned straightway to a fiery red.
"My children's heads are bare," said she,
"Exactly as they ought to be.
They all have over-active brains,
They couldn't live, but for my pains.
Now anyone who's not a fool,
Knows children's heads can't be too cool.
As for their throats, I keep them bare,
Because exposure to the air,
Is better far than all your care.
Diphtheria, scarlet fever, croup
Have never ventured near my troop.
Nor have they ever had the pain
Of inflammation on the brain.
All this is owing to my care
In having heads and throats go bare.
My system must and shall be right,
Whatever says my neighbor white.
As to my darlings' voices—well!
What would you have, I pray you tell?
Sweet are their voices, sweet and clear,
Delightful to their mother's ear."

"Well, well," said Mrs. Hen, "no doubt
You've said your say quite out and out.
I'm sure I've sense as well as you,
And know as well just what to do.
I keep my children safe from harm,
By covering heads and throats, so warm.
This keeps their brains and voices clear;
This makes their chirping sweet to hear.
Their health is owing to my care
In never letting them go bare.
You say your system must be right;
I say the same, with all my might."
    Turkey-hen
"Alas! I pity all your brood!"
    White hen
"I hope your grief will do you good!"
    Turkey-hen
"Their heads are hot.
Their throats are muffled."
    White hen
"And yours have tempers always ruffled!"
Turkey-hen
"Your children's legs are yellow. Fie!"
    White hen
"If they were red they'd better die!"
    Turkey-hen, to her brood
"My children, do not linger near;
Such language is not fit to hear."
    Little Turkeys

"We're going now, goodbye, young chicks!"
Little Chickens
"Goodbye, your legs look just like sticks!"

"Is that all?" asked Lou. "I wish there was some more. Do little turkeys really have bare necks and bare throats?"

"All the ones I ever saw did."

"What sort of noise do they make? I never saw any young turkeys."

"They make a pretty little whistling noise. But it's time for me to take my morning walk. Do you want to go with me?"

"I do, if you think we'll see any young turkeys."

"I don't think there are any very young turkeys at this time of year. People are fattening up those that were hatched last spring, for Thanksgiving."

"Then I don't want to go. May I go down to the study, and make houses out of books? Or no, a railroad! That's the thing!"

"Yes, but be careful not to use any new or nice books."

Chapter 4

Lou went down to the study and began to play. He knew which books he was allowed to use. Most of them were large books, in strong leather covers and were on the lower shelves, where he could reach them. The wise and good men who wrote those books didn't dream that the time would come when all their works were good for was building a railroad! The study was a very long room, and Lou stretched his track all the way across it. Just as it was done, Jacob and Joshua burst in. They had been to school, and were on their way home to dinner.

"Hi, Lou!"

"Hi, guys!"

"What happened to your nose and lip?" cried Jacob.

"Oh, I fell down on the ice."

"What are you doing now?"

"Oh, I'm making a railroad."

"What fun! I wonder if Father will let us have some of his books!" cried Joshua.

"Your father doesn't have half as many books as my father," replied Lou.

"Yes he does. He has enough to make a real railroad. And yours is only make-believe." There would have been a heated argument, ending with Jacob and Joshua running home and Lou declaring he was glad they were going, but the railroad looked too inviting. All three began to run over the whole length of it.

"Clear the track!" shouted Jacob.

"Look out for the locomotive!" cried Lou.

"There'll be a regular smash up!" said Joshua.

They jumped, they laughed, they ran. Never were there noisier, happier passengers on any railroad track in the world. Soon the door opened, and a serious face looked in. The boys stopped running and looked a little frightened.

"Do you care, Papa?" asked Lou. "We're playing railroad. Mama said I could."

"I think you'll have to clear the track now," said Papa. "The chief engineer wants to use the road." So Lou picked up the books and put them back in their places, and the other boys went home.

"What should I do now?" thought Lou. "I wish I had a ball. If I had a ball, I would always have something to do." He went to the kitchen to see if Abigail would make one for him. He found her getting dinner. Her sleeves were rolled up, and her face was very red.

"Don't come in here now," she said. "I'm too busy."

"Well, when you're not busy, will you make me a ball?"

"What's the use? You would lose it in five minutes."

"It wasn't my fault that I lost the last one," said Lou. "It got stuck on the roof of the barn. And the one before that disappeared somehow. I never knew where it went."

"That's just it. You lose balls faster than I can make them. Run along now. I can't have you here when I am making dinner. It distracts me, and I get too much salt in the gravy, or else don't put any in."

Lou went off very slowly. "Oh, I *wish* I had a ball!" he kept saying. "Or else a knife. If I had a knife, I could make lots of things."

He was very glad to find that his mama had come home. After she had taken off her coat, she said, "I thought I would stop on my way home and get something for you, because you had had such a fall. I couldn't find anything but this little red and white ball."

"Oh, thank you, Mama! I was just wishing I had a ball! I'm so glad!" He tossed it into the air, and it didn't come down again. "Hey, where is it?" he cried.

"I don't know. I didn't see where it went," said Mama. "How unlucky you always are with your balls! You lose them the first thing." Lou began to cry.

"It's not my fault," he said. "I only just tossed it up." After a long time, the ball was found perched on the top of an old wardrobe in the middle of lots of dust, some pamphlets, a few newspapers, and the pattern of a little jacket.

"Oh, *here* is the missing pattern!" said Mama. "I'm so glad! I thought it was lost."

"Aren't you glad I sent my ball up there to look for it?" said Lou.

Chapter 5

On Thanksgiving Day, Lou and his parents were invited to dinner at Uncle Arthur's. Abigail went home to spend the day with her mother and the house was locked up. Abigail took the key, because she was going to be home first. She had a basket on her arm full of things Lou's mama had given her for her mother. There was a chicken, some pies, a loaf of bread, and some apples.

There was a very long table in Uncle Arthur's dining room, because he had quite a few children, and those who were away had come home to spend this day. There wasn't room for the younger ones at this table, and they had a little one all to themselves. It was a long time before it was their turn to be served, and they amused themselves by watching what was going on, and chattering with each other.

"What are you going to have, Jacob?" asked Lou. "I'm going to have chicken, and then maybe I'll get the wishbone."

"I always have to have the drumstick," said Jacob. "The other boys always get the wishbones."

"There'll be five wishbones today," said Joshua. "There are five chickens in the pie. I heard Bridget say so."

"Then let's all have chicken pie!" said Lou. "Maybe we'll all get wishbones."

"Do we really get just what we wish for when we break the bone between us?" asked Jacob.

"Of course we do," said Lou.

"What did you ever get?"

"Once I got a live pony."

"Oh, what a story!" cried Jacob.

"I only said it for fun," said Lou. "I *wished* for a pony, anyhow."

"But you *said* you got one," persisted Jacob. "And that was wrong."

"It wasn't a down-upright lie," said Lou. "I only said it for fun."

"I think it was a down-upright lie," said Joshua.

Lou jumped down from his chair, and ran to his mama.

"Isn't a down-upright lie worse than a common lie?" he whispered in her ear. His mama looked at him in astonishment.

"No," she said, "all lies are the same, and all are bad. Lying is one of the worst things you could do."

"Jacob says I've lied," said Lou.

"And is that true, son?"

"No, Mama. I said I had a live pony, but I only said it for fun."

"There's nothing funny about saying something that's not true. Never say such things. And of all days in the year, don't choose this one for arguments."

Lou went back to his seat, feeling quite ashamed.

"What did aunty say?" asked Jacob.

"She said all lies are the same." But *I* think it would be much worse to say Jesus was the wickedest man in the world, than to say just for fun, that I had a pony."

The children's dinner was now brought to them. On this day they were all allowed to choose what they wanted. They always ate too much, and made themselves uncomfortable.

"I want chicken pie," said Lou.

"And so do I," said Jacob.

"Me too," said Joshua. .

"Oh, I've got a wishbone!" cried Joshua.

"And so have I!" said Lou.

"I don't. I've got two old drumsticks!" said Jacob, in an unhappy voice. "Papa! Do I *have* to have drumsticks on Thanksgiving Day?"

Everybody at the long table laughed at this, and Jacob's papa was kind enough to take back the drumsticks and search for a wishbone, which he soon found.

"Now we're all set," said Lou, and soon the three little bones were seen standing on their little legs in a row.

"What are you going to wish for, Lou?" asked Jacob.

"Oh, I know! But you can't tell what you wish for or you won't get your wish."

"I was going to wish Thanksgiving would come every day," said Joshua.

"Mama says she always used to wish to be good, when she had a wishbone," said Lou. "That's the reason she's so good now."

"She isn't any better than my mama," said Joshua.

"Oh yes she is."

"No she isn't." The two voices were now raised so high, that Lou's mama came to see what was the matter.

"Eat your dinner, like a good boy," she said, "and don't let me hear any more arguing today, not one word." By this time so many good things were sent to the children's table, that they became friends at once. They had a merry time together after dinner. A little old man came into the room on all fours crying out, "Who'll go a-nutting, a-nutting, a-nutting?" and as the children ran after him, nuts kept falling from a bag he carried on his back. He scampered upstairs and downstairs, through living rooms and halls and bedrooms, and all the children went wherever he went, laughing, and shouting, and picking up nuts, until they had to stop to catch their breath.

Then, when the uproar was over, they were taken to the living room, and shown an enormous bag, made of tissue paper, and suspended from the ceiling. This bag was full of different kinds of candies. Each child was blindfolded in turn, and allowed to hit at the bag with a long stick, to try to make a hole in it so that some of the candy could fall out. It was a long time before anyone broke through the paper, but when a hole was finally made, what fun there was! All sorts of nice things came rattling down upon their heads, and were snatched up by their nimble fingers, until at last the bag had given away all it had, and hung like a popped balloon, swinging in the air. Nobody enjoyed this fun more than the grownups who looked on, laughing at their children's merriment, and rejoicing to see them so happy.

Lou had his pockets so full of nuts that he could hardly walk, and his hands were so full of candy that he didn't know how to eat it.

"Mama, won't you keep my things for me?" he said. "What a nice time we are having! What a good old man that was, who gave us so many nuts!" His mama laughed, and said she didn't think the old man was very old. In fact, it was really one of Lou's cousins, dressed in some old clothes and with Grandma's glasses on his nose.

Chapter 6

WHEN THEY WENT home that evening, Lou's mama said that she wished she could get all *her* family together for Christmas dinner.

"Why don't you try?" said Papa.

"It's such a long trip to take in the middle of winter," she said. "I know Mother couldn't come. As for the uncles, I think they might all come. Then if Sammy would bring her baby, what great times we would have!" Mama looked so happy at the mere thought, that it made them all happy to see her.

"Would they all go home after dinner?" asked Lou, in a sleepy voice.

"Oh no, they would stay here a long time. At least Aunt Sammy would. Your uncles, I suppose, could only spare a few days."

Lou wanted to go right to bed. He carried his wishbone with him and put it under his pillow, together with a little paper bag of nuts and a pack of candies. Mama wrote letters all evening, in which she told all about Thanksgiving, and invited her family to come and spend the Christmas holidays with her. In a few days, answers came from them all. Grandma said she was getting too old to take trips in the winter. The four uncles said they would come, but only for a few days. Aunt Sammy said she would certainly come if her husband could come with her, but he couldn't. A few days later she wrote that she was coming after all, since her brothers promised to pick her up on their way.

Lou was very happy. He thought his uncles and his Aunt Sammy would tell him stories all day long. He was quite sure they would bring him Christmas presents, and wondered what these would be.

Mama had a lot to do. She tried to remember what her brothers liked best, and whether they slept on featherbeds or mattresses. Lou's little crib was brought down from the attic, where it had been stowed away with old furniture, and it was prepared for Aunt Sammy's baby. Abigail made plum puddings and mince pies, and all sorts of things, and helped prepare the beds. Lou liked to see so much going on. He tumbled into the middle of every bed, and got his hair full of down and feathers. He tasted the mincemeat to see if was good, and was everywhere at once. At last everything was ready, even down to a little vase of Mama's best flowers on the dresser of Aunt Sammy's room.

"Now," she said, "the sooner they come, the better! To think that I am going to see my dear Sammy's baby, and Sammy herself, and all the boys! I'm so happy I could cry!"

It was late in the afternoon the day before Christmas when the travelers arrived. Uncle Frank was carrying the baby, exactly as if she was his child, and it was his business to take care of her. The other uncles followed, with all sorts of bags and bundles. Last of all came Aunt Sammy, carrying nobody but herself. Lou's mama seized the baby just as Aunt Sammy had seized Lou, five and a half years ago, and unbuttoned her coat with just as eager hands. The baby was two years old now. She had large, dark eyes, dark brown hair, and held a ragdoll, nearly as big as herself, tightly in her arms.

"What a little darling!" said her Aunt Laura, who was Lou's mama. "What a beautiful child! Oh Sammy! Now you know how delightful it is to have a baby of your own!"

"I don't think I love her much more than I did Lou when he was a baby," said Aunt Sammy. "But the uncles make such a fuss over her, just as they did over him. I've hardly held her at all today! Lou, you sweet little boy, come and kiss your aunty once more. How he has grown! What do you think of your baby cousin, dear?"

"I don't think much of her," said Lou.

"Lou!" cried Mama, greatly embarrassed.

"I thought she would be big enough to play with me," explained Lou. "And she isn't anything but just a baby, holding another baby."

"One of these days she will be big enough," said Aunt Sammy.

"She's the best little thing I've ever seen," said Uncle Tom. "You can do whatever you want with her. Look at this." And they laid the baby on a small blanket, took the blanket by the four corners, and swung it back and forth saying, "Who wants to buy a sack of potatoes?"

Lou laughed at this sight until the tears rolled down his cheeks, and Mama said, "How can you let them do that, Sammy?"

"I can't help it," said Aunt Sammy. "I thought yesterday, that among them all they would kill her with such games."

"She likes it," said Uncle Robert. "Come here, you little beauty! Well Lou, do you like listening to stories as much as ever? You and I had fun times together when you were younger!"

But now it was time for tea, and it took a long time to find seats for everybody, and there was lots of laughing and joking until Lou's papa was ready to ask a blessing. Then they became quiet and serious. Aunt Sammy folded her baby's little hands together, for she had her seated next to her, and baby kept very still.

"What does baby eat?" asked Lou. "Does she eat her mama?"

Everybody laughed at this question, and it was awhile before Lou's little silver cup was brought full of milk for baby, who was very hungry. But she couldn't take time to eat, because she was so busy looking at Lou. Her mama finally had to take her away to a room by herself, so she would eat where there was nobody to distract her.

"Can't I stay up later than usual, tonight Mama?" asked Lou.

"No, darling. You know you're going to hang up your stocking tonight, and will want to be up very early to see what's in it."

"Yes I will! Will the baby hang up her stocking, too?"

"I guess we will hang one up for her. She's not old enough to do it herself."

"It must be a very little stocking," said Lou. "Was I as tiny as she is?"

"No, not at her age. You're a boy, you know, and boys are usually bigger than girls. Come on, let's ask Aunt Sammy to hang up a little stocking for baby; then you can put something in it."

"Yes I can!" cried Lou.

The baby lay fast asleep in Lou's crib, and her mama pinned her tiny stocking over it. Then Lou climbed up and dropped something into the stocking, his face full of joy.

"Oh what fun it is!" he cried. "When my little cousin wakes up tomorrow morning, how glad she'll be! May I put in something else, Aunty?"

"Yes, put in any old toy you're tired of. It will be new to her and make her just as happy as new ones."

So Lou filled the little stocking with some of his little toys, and then he hung up his own and went to bed. As soon as he was asleep, they all came on tiptoe to his room with their Christmas gifts. The stocking was soon so full that it could stand up by itself. Uncle Robert put his present for Lou on the dresser. It was a large box full of railroad cars that Lou had wanted for a long time. Uncle Frank put a set of Rollo books into the little bookshelf. Uncle Tom had brought a warehouse, with little barrels and bags to hoist up and be stored away in it. Uncle Fred put a very large box of wooden animals at the foot of the bed.

They all laughed to think how surprised and happy Lou would be in the morning, but they had to laugh very softly so they didn't wake him up. Then someone suggested that everybody hang up a stocking, which made plenty of fun for the rest of the evening.

Chapter 7

Lou awoke before it was light, and since he couldn't see his stocking, he felt it and tried to guess what was in it. *"It's full to the top!"* he thought. *"I wish it was daylight."* As he reached out of bed to lay it in the chair by his side, his hand bumped against the box of animals. "Hey, what's this?" he cried. He jumped out of bed and felt the box, as he had felt his stocking. But he began to shiver because it was a very cold morning, and had to get back in bed, carrying the box with him. He opened it, and took out a dog.

"What can this be?" he said. "It feels like a lamb or else a horse. No, the tail is not a horse's tail. It must be a cow. No, it isn't a cow; it has no horns. Maybe it's a dog. Yes, it *is* a dog." He took out one animal after another, feeling them all over. "I'm glad I'm not blind," he thought. "Blind people must go feeling everything, and get very tired of feeling."

"Lou," said his papa, opening the door gently, "I wish you a Merry Christmas. And I wish you would stop talking. It is only three o'clock, and none of us want to get up so early. Lie down, close your eyes, and go to sleep." He closed the door, and went back to his own bed in the next room.

"I'll lie down, but I won't shut my eyes and I won't go to sleep," said Lou to himself. "It's three o'clock, and that's almost six. And at six I can get up." He lay down and began to think of his presents. The next thing he knew it was getting light, and he could see objects quite well. He grabbed his stocking, and one by one, took out all the things in it. They were all small, but he was happy with everything. Then he took the animals from the box, and stood them up all over his bed. He was quite covered with them when he spied the warehouse.

"Oh! Oh! Oh! A real house! With real windows! Move, animals, move quickly, and let me get out of bed!" he cried. Hearing his voice, his mama opened the door and peeked in. She was only half dressed.

"Oh Mama! I wish you a Merry Christmas! See what nice things these are! Look at my animals! Look at my house!"

"Yes, love. But you must get dressed before you look at anything else," said his mama. "Come, your bath is ready."

Lou wished that he didn't have to take a bath, but it was soon over, and so was getting dressed. He could put on his own shoes and socks now, and dress himself almost entirely. By the time breakfast was ready he was almost crazy. So many wonderful presents coming all at once quite overwhelmed him. Uncle Tom showed him how to hoist up his goods into his warehouse, and he was so delighted that he could hardly look at his other things.

"I won't be a stagecoach driver when I'm grown up," he said. "I'll have a big warehouse and hoist up goods. What will I be then?"

"A merchant," said Uncle Tom. But merchants don't hoist up goods themselves. It's very hard work and they hire men to do it."

"Maybe they'll hire me, when I grow up," said Lou. "I don't think it is hard work."

Aunt Sammy came in now, leading her baby by the hand.

"Here comes Baby," said Lou. "I'll show my presents to her. Seems to me she ought to have a name. Isn't she big enough?"

"Yes, of course," said her mama. "She has a name. It's Sammy. But we have always called her Baby, because my name is Sammy too."

"We could call her Sam," said Uncle Robert. "It's just about long enough for such a little atom."

"Okay, Baby, your name is Sam now! Do you hear, my love?"

"Baby do hear Mama," said a little soft voice, as sweet as the cooing of a dove.

"Little girls are so sweet," said Uncle Frank, and he took the baby tenderly in his arms. She leaned her head against his chest, and sat quietly all through prayers.

There had been a lot of quiet fun going on in the house that Lou didn't know about. The grownups had all hung up their stockings, and had played funny tricks on each other with the odd things they put in them. They were indeed a happy and a joyous Christmas gathering; happy loving each other, and yet even more so in loving Jesus, whose birthday they were celebrating and who had given them reason to rejoice and be glad.

Chapter 8

AFTER BREAKFAST, LOU showed all his presents to little Sam, and she let him see hers. She had a lot, because each of the uncles had brought something for her, and so had Aunt Laura and Uncle James. The present that she liked best was a doll. It is true she had several already, but little girl mamas are like grown up, real mamas. They can make room in their hearts and in their arms for just as many babies as are given them. If you're the fifth or sixth or seventh little boy or girl in your family, you're just as welcome there as if you were the first or the only one. And so it will be in heaven. When you go there the gates will be opened as wide to let you in as if heaven were not already full of happy men and women and children! And the angels will greet you with songs as joyful as if all they were created for was to rejoice over *you*!

Lou didn't know how to talk to Sam very well. He had never been with little children. He thought he should talk baby talk. "Does 'itty Sam want to see Lou's horses and dogs? Does she want to hold them in her 'ittle arms? She can!"

"Oh Lou! Don't talk like that," said his mama. "Sam will understand you fine if you talk the same as you do to other people."

"I thought you said that I must be very gentle with her, Mama," said Lou.

"Yes, I did say so. But you can be gentle and loving without being silly."

Just then, Jacob and Joshua came in, eager to see Lou's presents and to show him theirs. But the moment they spied little Sam, they stopped caring about the toys. They sat down on the carpet, put her between them, and felt her soft arms and neck with surprise and delight.

"Look at those boys!" said little Sam's mama. "I never saw anything so funny! They all want to hold her.

"Yes, they are very affectionate boys," said Laura.

"My baby is the most loving little girl in the world," said Aunt Sammy. "Come here, my little lamb, and give Mama one of your sweet little hugs." Baby Sam ran at once into her mama's arms. She laid her little round cheek upon her breast and cuddled down in her embrace as a young bird does in its nest, under its mother's wing. Then she got up on her knees and put her arms around her mama's neck, and kissed her five, ten, twenty times.

Lou's mama laughed. "I must admit," she said, "that even Lou wouldn't do more than that."

"The whole thing makes me envious," said Uncle Robert. "I wish I had a baby so I could feel such little arms around my neck. Hey! It's snowing! What large flakes!"

"I'm glad," said Lou. "I hope it will snow and snow and snow and block up all the roads, so that you will all have to stay here forever and ever."

"That's not very likely to happen," replied his uncle. "We have to go home to our work. Your mama would soon get tired of seeing four big men lounging around."

However, it kept on snowing steadily. Finally, Jacob and Joshua had to wade home through the storm, in snow nearly up to their chins. But they were used to it and didn't care.

"As for me, I *like* to eat my Christmas dinner in a snowstorm," said Uncle Frank, as they seated themselves at the table. "The difference between this warm room and what is going on outside is so nice."

While one of her uncles was asking a blessing, little Sam opened her eyes and saw quite near her, a dish of beets. She had never seen any before, and she thought they were very pretty; they were so red. So she reached over and took a whole one, and laid it on her plate. When the blessing ended and Lou opened his eyes and saw the beet on little Sam's plate, and her serious, innocent face, he couldn't help laughing.

"Look, Mama! Look, Papa! Look, Aunty!" he cried, in his quick way. Everybody looked and everybody laughed, and so the Christmas dinner began amid cheerful faces.

Meanwhile, the soft white snowflakes kept flying down. They landed with noiseless footsteps on the fences and perched on the housetop. Some balanced themselves nicely on the branches of the trees until they bent under their weight. Some danced up against the side of the stable, and when they had made a layer of pure snow, new flakes came down and covered them. Each one was perfect in itself. Each one was worthy to be caught and preserved forever, if it would only agree to stay. But they didn't want to be caught, and they didn't know how beautiful they were, and so they flung themselves around here and there and played with each other in the air. Some of them settled down on the windowsill of the dining room, and watched the cheerful company at the Christmas dinner. But they didn't want to go into that warm room, pleasant though it was. They liked to stay out in the cold and would have fainted away if they had been forced to stay in the warm, even for a few minutes.

"Do you have any poor people around here, Laura?" asked one of her brothers.

"Yes, I guess there are poor people everywhere. It says so in the Bible, and I suppose God intended them to keep us from becoming utterly selfish. However, I don't think there is any real suffering here. A man can get a snug little house with a little land for very low rent. He can raise a pig and grow his own vegetables. This morning I sent a large chicken pie to Mrs. Medill, Becky's mother, and she sent back word that I was very polite!"

"By the way, what happened to Becky? I remember you used to write home some funny things about her."

"She's living with Mrs. Carson, at Meadeville. She's quite happy there, and Mrs. Carson is bringing her up extremely well."

"Mrs. Medill gives me a good deal of trouble still. She is constantly borrowing things, which of course she never returns. One day it's a little flour, another day a little soap, the next a cup of molasses. It's so annoying. But let me tell you the funniest story about Mrs. Simpson, another poor woman I've been helping. She sent a little girl over a few weeks ago to borrow our family Bible. I asked the girl if her mother had no Bible of her own. She said she had one, but it had no place in it for recording deaths, and since she had just lost a child, she wanted to make a note of it in ours."

"Oh, that is too ridiculous to be true!" cried Uncle Tom, while all the rest had to stop eating their dinner in order to have a good laugh. And while they laughed, the white snowflakes looked in at the window, and knew they would make it impossible for any of them to travel home next day.

Chapter 9

"There is a gigantic snowdrift in the yard," said Uncle Tom. "If we were younger, we would want to make a house for ourselves in it."

"It wouldn't hurt you old men to make one now," said Lou's mama. "Respected as you are, you need some sort of exercise, and with all that snow on the roads, walking is out of the question."

"Ah, you want to get us out of the way, so that you and Sammy can have each other all to yourselves. Well, what do you say, Bob? A house, or no house?"

"A house, of course. Anything is better than lounging around all day. Come on, Frank. Come on, Fred. Grab your shovels and let's go."

"We'll make you a snow palace, Lou!" said Uncle Fred. "A palace fit for a king, just like we used to make every winter."

"A real house?" cried Lou. "Can I watch you make it?"

"Sure, if you can take the cold."

"It won't be good for him to stand still and watch you, he'll get too cold," said his mama. "You'll have to give him some work to do."

"He can cart away the snow we dig out," said Uncle Tom. "Or drag it away on his sled."

So they all set to work. The snowdrift was on the side of the stable, and was about twelve feet high! It lay there in the sunshine, pure and beautiful. The first thing Lou's uncles did was cut a door in one end. Then they kept digging out the snow from the inside, just as you scrape out an apple core. They threw this snow out, and Lou filled a box with it that was tied to his sled. When he had dragged it away and was ready to dump it out, one of his uncles had to help him. It was hard work for them all, and they were very hungry when they were called in to lunch, and tired too. But by that time there was room for them all inside the snow house.

After lunch they finished it. It was big enough to hold eight or ten people! They spread a piece of carpet over the floor and made benches all around the sides with loose boards that they found in the stable. Lou was so delighted that he hardly knew what to say or what to do.

"Now before you start living in your house, Lou," said Uncle Frank, "you need a fire. You would freeze to death without a fire."

"Mama won't let me play with fire," said Lou. "Once, I almost set the house on fire."

"She'll let us play with it," said his uncle. "Is there an old stove anywhere? We had a stove in our snow palaces."

"There's a little one up in the attic," said Lou. "It's old and rusty, and it's small."

"The smaller the better," said his uncle. "Come, show us how to get to the attic."

Lou led the way, stamping up the stairs with eager feet. Two of his uncles carried down the stove, while another grabbed an old roll of carpeting.

"What can those boys be doing?" said Lou's mama. "I never heard such a racket. And Lou seems nearly wild."

The little stove was soon placed in the middle of the snow house, a hole was cut in the roof for the pipe to pass through, and a bright fire began to spread wonderful warmth around. The old carpeting was then spread from the snow palace to the kitchen door, and Lou was sent to call his mama and aunty to walk over it.

"It seems like only yesterday that we were called out just like this to admire their handiwork," said Aunt Sammy. "Remember how many palaces like this they used to make when they were little boys? Should I take little Sam?"

"Wrap her up well and she'll be fine," said Lou's mama.

Lou trembled with joy as he led his mama along over the path of carpeting to his beautiful white palace. No polished marble ever made its owner more joyful.

"This is really delightful!" said his mama. "Tomorrow you can invite Jacob and Joshua, and Willy Lee and Georgie Merton to come and have lunch here with you. At that time of day it won't be very cold, and you'll enjoy yourselves so much you'll never forget it."

For an answer, Lou threw himself on the floor of his snow palace and rolled all the way across it like a ball. His uncles felt well repaid for all the work they had done, and said they wished they could stay to see the lunch party the next day.

Little Sam, meanwhile, looked about her with great surprise. She went and sat on all the benches, and kept touching the snow walls with her little pink fingers, until they became quite red. One of her uncles lifted her up to touch the ceiling, and a shower of snow came falling down into her face and eyes. She shuddered and shook her head, but didn't cry.

"What a sweet little thing!" said Aunt Laura. "Let's go back to the living room with her. Come on, Lou. Your fire is almost out and it's getting late."

"I wish I could stay here all night," said Lou. "Do I *have* to go in now?"

"Yes, it's getting cold now, and it will soon be dark."

"I am afraid my house will melt away in the night," said Lou.

"It won't melt day or night while this cold weather lasts," said Uncle Frank.

They went back to the living room together, and Lou began to play again with his new toys. Little Sam sat with her new doll in her arms and watched him. She didn't know what to make of him. He wasn't a baby like herself, and he wasn't a man like her papa; what was he then? How serious she looked, sitting on the floor among the toys, pondering this tricky question in her little bit of a head!

Early the next morning before daylight, the four uncles went away. They left behind a little package for Lou that his grandma had sent him. They had forgotten to give it to him on Christmas day. It was a whole lot of warm socks and mittens that his grandma had knitted for him, and Lou's mama was very glad to have them. But Lou had never known what it was like to not have either mittens or socks, so he didn't appreciate these.

"I would think Grandma would have known better than to send me such things," he said, looking quite red.

His mama didn't answer. She knew that he was too young to understand that it costs a great deal more love to knit, knit, knit for little boys, than to step into a toyshop and buy the toys made by other hands.

Lou missed his uncles very much. They had spent nearly all their time playing with him or working for him, and after they left, he didn't like to play alone. But he could now read his Rollo books well enough to enjoy them, and they kept him busy and happy when he was tired of playing with his toys.

Chapter 10

At last Aunt Sammy and little Sam had to go home, too. Uncle Henry came for them, and drove them away. The baby's crib was put away in the attic again. The room in which Aunt Sammy had slept was put in order and everything went back to normal. Lou had his lessons every morning and every afternoon, just as he did before the holidays. He read aloud to his mama, had a few words to spell, and a few sentences to write.

So the rest of the winter passed quietly away, and spring came smiling in, as sure of a welcome as you are, when you go with a pleasant, shining face to your mama. Lou's snow-palace had long since melted away, and flown up into the skies to make pure white clouds. Grass and flowers were springing up everywhere, and Lou's papa and mama once more could work in their garden. Lou was now nearly six years old, and was a helpful little boy. He could get the letters from the Post Office, and mail those written by his papa and mama. He could trundle away all the weeds thrown into the garden paths, and even weed some of the beds himself. He also had a little garden of his own, but he only worked in that once in a while.

When Abigail wanted to make pudding and needed milk and eggs, Lou could get them for her, sometimes in one place, and sometimes in another. He grew happier and better every day, for there is nothing in the world that makes us as happy as being useful. Grownups who live for nothing except to please themselves, and have as good a time in the world as they can, are never really happy. Things are constantly happening to annoy and trouble them, and then they complain and grumble. Even little children are made by their Creator so that they cannot lie down to sleep in sweet peace at night if, during the day, they have done nothing kind for anyone around them. The next time you go to bed, unhappy and worried, ask yourself who you have tried hardest to please all day: yourself or your neighbor or your dear Father in heaven. And remind yourself ten, twenty times a day, "Even Christ did not please Himself."[13]

---

[13] For even Christ did not please Himself; but as it is written, "The reproaches of those who reproached You fell on Me." Romans 15:3

Chapter 11

Lou had a little friend who he liked very much. They didn't get to play together often, because Walter lived on a farm outside of the village. When they visited each other, they stayed several days at a time, and thus learned to know and love each other's mamas. It was Lou's turn to visit Walter's this year, and he was very glad to go, not only because he loved Walter so much, but also because there are lots of activities that only happen on a farm. He liked to hunt for eggs, and feed the poultry, and follow the men when they cut the hay and raked it. He even helped rake a little himself. And then it was such fun when the hay was piled up high in the carts, to ride to the barn on the top with Walter by his side. Walter's mama liked to see them so happy together, and she was always very gentle and loving toward them both.

When Lou went home after his visit this year, he said to his mama, "Do you think you will ever die, dear Mama?"

"What a question!" said Mama. "Yes, of course I'll die, sometime."

"If you do, I hope Papa will marry Walter's mama. I love her so much, and she is so sweet and kind. And then I would have a brother. Walter would be my very own brother."

His mama laughed. "What would Walter's papa say to such an arrangement? He would be left all alone."

"Yes, but I don't think he would care. He would know I needed somebody for a mama."

It was only a few days after this that Walter's papa came driving up to the door, looking very serious and anxious.

"My wife is very sick," he said to Lou's mama, "and I would be glad to have you drive over with me to see her. She thinks she is not going to get well, and has something to say to you about our little boy." Mrs. James got ready to go right away. As she did so, her tears fell fast, and Lou followed her silently, trying not to get in her way or annoy her with questions.

"I'll be just as good as I can while you're gone," he whispered as she left the door.

"Poor Walter! Poor Walter!" he thought. "If his mama dies what *will* he do?"

Lou's mama didn't come back that night. He felt very lonely and sad until his papa came in from evening prayers and comforted and entertained him. The next day he sat at the window and watched every carriage that drove by. Now and then he ran up the road to see if his mama were coming. Late in the afternoon, when he had quit watching, she came quietly in. She caught Lou in her arms, and held him close to her heart. She tried not to cry while she said, "Walter's dear, sweet mama has gone to heaven. She was very glad to go, so you must not cry." But Lou burst into a flood of tears, and threw himself upon the floor and hid his face.

His mama comforted him as well as she could. "Dying seems dreadful to you now, my darling," she said. "But that is because you don't know how God's own children love to go where their own dear Father is. Walter's mama was sorry to leave her precious little boy, but she loved Jesus even more than she loved him. And she knew He would comfort her lonely child."

"Oh Mama! I wish I was just as old as you!"

"Then I couldn't hold you in my arms like I am now," said his mama, drawing him closer to her.

"No," said Lou, his voice trembling, "but then I would die just when you did."

"And why do you want to when I do, darling?"

"Because I don't want to live after you're dead." He leaned his head upon his mama's shoulder and cried bitterly.

"None of us can choose when we will die, or how. If we really love God, we will be willing to have Him choose for us. Perhaps you will die before I do, and then I shall not have any dear little boy to love. But if you do, I won't say that I want to die because you're dead. I'll say that I want to live or die just as God wishes."

"Mama, do you think I love God?"

"I hope you do. It seems hardly possible that you can help loving my best Friend."

"Do you love Him very much, Mama?"

"Yes, I do. Not as much as I should, but very much."

"Better than Papa?"

"Oh yes."

"Then I plan to love Him, too. How can I find out whether I do love Him, really and truly?"

"I don't suppose that while you're a little boy, you'll feel just as I do. But if you really love Him you will always be trying to please Him. You will be faithful about your lessons, whether I am watching you or not. You will try to cure yourself of contradicting and arguing and getting angry. You will speak the truth, no matter what it costs. And all these things will make you happy. You will go on, as long as you live, growing happier and happier every day. And at last, when God has nothing more for you to do in this world, He will take you to live with Him in one of His mansions."

"What kind of a mansion will it be?"

"I don't know. You can be sure of one thing, however. It will be exactly what you will like best." Lou wiped away his tears, and his face grew bright again.

"Will Walter's mother have one, too?"

"Of course. Perhaps she won't have one all to herself. Perhaps there will be room in it for Walter and his papa and the two dear little girls of theirs who went to heaven when you were a baby. And now I have something else to tell you that you are going to like. Walter's mama, before she died, asked me to take care of him for her, during the next few years. She thinks he will be too lonely without her, and that he would be quite happy with us. His papa is willing to let him go because he has very little time to spend at home."

Lou clapped his hands and began to dance about the room. "We must be very kind to Walter," continued his mama. "We must never forget that he is a motherless little boy. And we must be patient with him if, at first, he seems sad and sorrowful and unhappy. Dear little fellow! I wanted to bring him home with me, but of course his papa needs him right now."

"Mama, Walter is a real good boy. I'm so glad he's coming to live here! Then you will have two little sons to weed your garden, and run errands for you."

"Yes," said Mama, "and I'll have four little feet to look after, instead of two."

"Do you mean that you will have more socks to mend?"

"No, I mean that I will have two boys to keep out of mischief, instead of one."

"I know one boy that is not going to trouble you anymore, Mama." His mama kissed him, and then his papa came home, and wanted to hear all about the death of Walter's mama. Lou went out into the garden and sat down under a tree. He felt both sad and happy.

Chapter 12

WHEN WALTER CAME to live with Lou, he brought with him two Bibles, exactly alike. They were his mama's parting gift to him and Lou. "I'm very glad to get this Holy Bible," said Lou, reading the gilt letters on the front of his. "I never had anything but a reverence Bible, before."

"A reference Bible, you mean," said his papa. "Your old Bible is just like your new one, only it has two columns of references in it."

"I like this best, anyhow," said Lou. "The letters are bigger and the cover is red. I like red covers. And besides, it's just like Walter's."

Walter seemed very gentle and pleasant. He followed Lou's mama around everywhere, and wanted her to talk to him about his own dear mama. When he had been there a few days, his papa drove over to see him, and brought him a little tent that he had ordered in Boston for the two boys. It was pitched in the orchard, and they played and read in it, and hung pictures cut from paper around the sides.

One afternoon they played that they were soldiers, and this tent was the only place they had to sleep in. They marched into the house and Lou said to his mama, "We are two soldiers who have lost our backpacks and everything but our tent. We have no blankets to sleep in, and no food to eat. Will you lend us some blankets, and give us some food, ma'am?"

"I will lend you some blankets, and give you some food, sir," replied Mrs. James. "But you look like very young soldiers to camp out. How about sleeping in my house tonight?"

"Thank you, ma'am," said Walter, "but we're not as young as we look. We must learn to bear hardships since we're soldiers." Lou's mama smiled, and gave them each a blanket, and enough food for their supper. The two soldiers went off to their tent and ate all she had given them with good appetites. Then when it began to grow dark, each knelt down and prayed to God, rolled himself in his blanket, and lay down to sleep. After a while, Lou lifted up his head and looked at Walter.

"Are you asleep, Walter?" he asked.

"No, are you?"

"I can't get to sleep because I don't have a pillow."

"Yes, and I feel things crawling on me," said Walter.

"What kind of things?"

"Spiders. They get into my ears, too."

"It's getting real dark."

"Yes. And it's cold."

"Listen! Don't you hear something?"

"Yes. What can it be? I wish our guns were loaded."

"Or else that we had a big cannon at the door of our tent. Don't you think this ground is quite hard?"

"Yes, and it's lonely out here. Do you suppose everybody has gone to bed?"

"Oh yes, it must be midnight, it's so dark. Listen! What was that?"

"Well boys," said a voice at the entrance of the tent, "are you almost ready to come in and go to bed?"

"Papa! Is that you?" cried Lou, jumping up. "We can't get to sleep, and the spiders get on us, and we don't have any pillows, and it is cold, and—"

"And you've camped out long enough? Very well, if you're fighting on the right side, I'll see if I can find a bed for you in my house."

"We are good soldiers, sir," said Walter.

They all went to the house together, where they were greatly surprised to see Lou's mama, sitting at her little table writing a letter.

"Mama! Are you up at this time of night?" cried Lou.

"Why not?" asked Mama, looking at the clock. Lou looked, too. He saw that it wasn't quite 9:15.

"Hey, we thought it was midnight!" he said.

"And now, boys, off to bed with you," said Lou's papa. They were glad enough to go. They had had quite as much camping out as they could stand. They undressed and jumped into bed, and were fast asleep when Lou's mama came, five minutes later, to take away their candle. When they awoke the next morning, and found themselves in their own little beds, they were very much astonished. The last thing they remembered was lying in the tent.

"Hey! How did we come here?" cried Lou.

"Your papa must have brought us in our sleep," said Walter. "Listen! The clock in the hall is striking. Let me count. Why, Lou! It's eight o'clock!"

"Oh, now I remember," said Lou. "We camped out until 9:15 last night, and then Papa made us come in. I wish he had let us camp out all night."

"So do I," said Walter. "It wasn't very cold."

"And the ground wasn't very hard."

"And it didn't matter if we didn't have pillows."

"And the spiders didn't hurt us."

"I wasn't afraid of anything, were you?"

"Not at all. It was too bad that Papa made us come in. Well! We'll camp out all night, next time."

"Yes. But not tonight."

"Oh no, not tonight." And that was the end of the matter from that time on. Neither of the boys was anxious to repeat the experiment. When they went downstairs, they found that breakfast was over, long ago. Abigail had kept some for them, and they went into the kitchen to eat it.

"Hold out your plate, and I'll give you some butter, Walter," said Lou. Walter did, and the moment Lou touched the plate, it broke in two.

"Oh no! Now, what will Mama say?" cried Lou.

"*I* didn't break it," said Walter.

"I'm sure I didn't either," said Lou.

"You don't need to look so scared," said Abigail. "The plate was cracked before."

"Who cracked it?"

"Oh, I don't know. I suppose someone put it into water that was too hot."

"It must have been you, then."

"Not me. I'm very careful how I treat your mama's plates. I wish you were half as careful as I am. You never brush your feet, and it takes half my time to scour the doors because you leave fingerprints on them so often."

"They aren't my fingerprints," said Lou.

"And you leave your boots and shoes lying about for me to pick up," continued Abigail.

"That isn't any worse than you washing all the buttons off the shirts," cried Lou. "Mama says she has to sew on so many buttons."

"*I* don't wash them off, they come off themselves," said Abigail. "Go on, eat your breakfast like a good boy, as Walter does. Dear me! I do wish somebody would oil the hinges of this door!"

"Why don't you do it yourself?"

"I don't have time. It takes all my time to hunt up things you've lost, and clean up the mud you bring in on your feet, and shut the doors after you, and put away what you leave lying around. Where's the last issue of *The Penny Magazine*? Your papa has been looking high and low for it."

"I don't know. I haven't had it," said Lou in a rather sullen tone.

"I know a poem about Mr. Nobody," said Walter, who wanted to make peace between the two of them. "Do you want to hear it?"

"Yes, I do," said Abigail.

Walter rose from the table, put his hands behind him, and began.

MR. NOBODY
I know a funny little man,
As quiet as a mouse,
Who does the mischief that is done
In everybody's house.
There's no one ever sees his face,
And yet we all agree,

> That every plate we break, was cracked
> By Mr. Nobody.
>
> 'Tis he who always tears our books,
> Who leaves the doors ajar;
> He pulls the buttons from our shirts,
> And scatters pins afar.
> That squeaking door will always squeak,
> For prithee, don't you see?
> We leave the oiling to be done
> By Mr. Nobody.
>
> He puts damp wood upon the fire
> That kettles cannot boil;
> His are the feet that bring in mud,
> And all the carpets soil.
> The papers always are mislaid;
> Who had them last, but he?
> There's no one tosses them about
> But Mr. Nobody.
>
> The finger-marks upon the doors
> By none of us are made;
> We never leave the blinds unclosed.
> To let the curtains fade.
> The ink we never spill; the boots
> That lying round you see,
> Are not our boots! They all belong
> To Mr. Nobody!

By this time both Abigail and Lou had recovered their good moods. Abigail really loved Lou dearly, and she didn't like anyone to find fault with him but herself. And Lou loved Abigail, and now that he was trying hard to be a good boy, he never made her angry her on purpose.

CHAPTER 13

THE TWO BOYS NOW went in search of Lou's mama. They found her at work in her garden, collecting seeds.

"Can we help, Mama?" cried Lou.

"You may, if you'll be careful not to get my seeds mixed up together."

"We'll be very careful," said Walter. "Oh, what tiny little seeds these are! And what a lot there are!"

"Isn't it wonderful that so many seeds come from one flower!" said Mrs. James. "Let me tell you a fable about that.

※※※※※※※※※※

There were once several plants growing in a field together. It was in the autumn, when most flowers are done blooming and have gone to seed. A sharp north wind came blustering along.

"Well, old ladies," he said, "You don't have much more time to live. What have you got to show as the fruit of the time you have spent on the earth?"

"He calls *us* old ladies," said Mrs. Marigold, turning quite yellow.

"And we are far younger than he is," cried Mrs. Dandelion.

"I don't have much to say," she replied. "I haven't idled away my life, however. In one brief summer, I've borne ten flowers, and each of these flowers now has two thousand six hundred seeds. So my children will be scattered all over this and many other fields, and go on keeping up our family name forever."

"As for me," said Mrs. Dandelion, "I've led a busy life, also. I've borne so many flowers that I haven't had time to count them. Each of these flowers has sent flying through the air three thousand winged seeds. They will spring up when

I'm gone, by the wayside and in the field. They will smile in the faces of children, and a million human beings will be made glad by them."

"And I," said Mrs. Thistle, "have nourished more than twenty soft blossoms. I am rough to the touch, but I am the mother of flowers of delicate silk. And each of my dear ones has filled the air with flying down. Each has flown, on twenty thousand wings, to start so many new families on the face of the earth."

"Men speak lovingly of me," said Mrs. Daisy, "I don't know why. I never try to make them notice me, and I cherish my family near the ground, so as to be out of sight. I've had twenty children this summer, and each is ready to give to the earth thirteen thousand seeds, and more. Wherever they spring up, they will be welcomed, and perhaps thirteen thousand lips will greet them with pleasure."

"You're too modest, little neighbor," said Mrs. Poppy. "You should lift your head higher, as I do mine. However, none of you have such a record as I can show. I've borne forty children, and each of them has produced fifty thousand seeds. They will spring up all over this and other lands. The fields of France will blush with them; they will breathe the air of Italy, and redden the highways of Switzerland. Call us "old ladies" if you will, Mr. North Wind. But you're far, far older than we, and what can you say, compared with what we say?"

"I can say this," said the North Wind. "It is I who take the seeds you have not power to scatter over the earth, and bear them on my wings to every region and into every climate. Without me, Mrs. Thistle, where would be your flying swarm? Without me, Mrs. Dandelion, how could yours find their way to three thousand homes? But now your hour has come. Your work is ended. Prepare to die." He breathed upon them, and they sank, one by one, below him. But their work lived long after they were dead; not one of them had worked in vain."

"I would like to hear Mrs. Dandelion talk," said Lou. "I don't think any of your flowers have so many seeds as the plants in your fable had."

"No, I don't think so either. But I want you and Walter to remember that every good word you speak, every right thing you do, is the little seed you sow. After a while it will spring up and bear fruit for God."

"I don't understand," said Walter.

"Perhaps I can't make you understand all I mean. But this is a part of it. "When you do a right thing and speak a good word, other children who see and hear you are likely to imitate you. And when they imitate you, their good words and deeds are the fruit of yours." By this time the boys wanted to go and play. So they ran off, chasing each other through the garden walks, under the trees, among the winding paths, past the orchard, and far out of sight. Lou's mama stopped working, and looked after them until they disappeared. "Dear little boys! How I love them!" she thought. "May God help me to sow seeds in their hearts that will spring up and bear fruit for His glory, a hundredfold!"

Walter stayed with Lou and his mama for three years. At the end of that time, his papa found a new mama for him, and took him home. But he was allowed to visit Lou for several long visits every year, and Lou went to the farm quite as often, so that they remained as good friends as ever. I cannot tell you anything more about Lou, because his mama's journal, in which she wrote down his sayings and doings until he was about six years old, stops here. Perhaps it is just as well. If there were any more books about him, you might get tired of him.

Appendix

My Mother

Who fed me from her gentle breast,
And hushed me in her arms to rest,
And on my cheek sweet kisses pressed?
My Mother.

When sleep forsook my open eye,
Who was it sung sweet hushaby,
And rocked me that I would not cry?
My Mother.

Who sat and watched my infant head,
When sleeping in my cradle bed,
And tears of sweet affection shed?
My Mother.

When pain and sickness made me cry,
Who gazed upon my heavy eye
And wept for fear that I should die?
My Mother.

Who dressed my doll in clothes so gay,
And taught me pretty how to play.
And minded all I had to say?
My Mother.

Who taught my infant lips to pray,
And love God's holy book and day.
And walk in Wisdom's pleasant way?
My Mother.

And can I ever cease to be
Affectionate and kind to thee,
Who was so very kind to me?
My Mother

Ah, no! The thought I cannot bear;
And if God please my life to spare,
I hope I shall reward thy care,
My Mother.

Who ran to help me when I fell,
And would some pretty story tell,
Or kiss the place to make it well?
My Mother.

When thou art feeble, old, and gray,
My healthy arm shall be thy stay,
And I will soothe thy pains away.
My Mother.

And when I see thee hang thy head,
'Twill be my turn to watch thy bed.
And tears of sweet affection shed,
My Mother.

For God, who lives above the skies,
Would look with vengeance in His eyes,
If I should ever dare despise
My Mother.

[Taylor later softened the last verse, changing it to the following.*]

For could our Father in the skies
Look down with pleased or loving eyes,
If ever I could dare despise
My Mother.

Ann Taylor (1782-1866)
* Note from Mamalisa.com

A Glimpse at Elizabeth Prentiss

In attempting to sum up the characteristics of her writings, her husband George Prentiss wrote the following:

First, and most prominent, was their *purpose*. Her pen moved always and only under a sense of *duty*. She held her talent as a gift from God, and consecrated it sacredly to the enforcement and diffusion of His truth. If I may quote once more the words of her publisher in his tribute to her memory—"her great desire and determination to educate in the highest and best schools was never overlooked or forgotten. She never, like many writers of religious fiction, caught the spirit of sensationalism that is in the air, or sought for effects in unhealthy portraiture, corrupt style, or unnatural combinations."

Second, she was *unconventional*. Her writings were not religious in any stereotyped, popular sense. Her characters were not stenciled. The holiest of them were strongly and often amusingly individualized. She did not try to make automatons to repeat religious commonplaces, but actual men and women, through whose very peculiarities the Holy Spirit revealed His presence and work.

Third, I have already referred to her *sprightliness*. [in a previous section.] She had naturally a keen sense of humor which overflowed both in her conversation and in her books. She saw nothing in the nature of the faith she professed which bade her lay violent hands on this propensity; and she once said that if her religion could not stand her saying a funny thing now and then it was not worth much. But, whatever she might say or write of this character, one never felt that it betrayed any irreverent lightness of spirit. The undertone of her life was so deeply reverential, so thoroughly pervaded with adoring love for Christ, that it made itself felt through all her lighter moods, like the ground-swell of the sea through the sparkling ripples on the surface.

Fourth, her style was easy, colloquial, never stilted or affected, marked at times by an energy and incisiveness which betrayed earnest thought and intense feeling. She aimed to impress the truth, not her style, and therefore aimed at plainness and directness. Her hard common sense, of which her books reveal a goodly share, was offset by her vivid fancy which made even the region of fable tributary to the service of truth.

Fifth, her books were intensely *personal*; expressions, I mean, of her own experience. Many of her characters and scenes are simple transcripts of fact, and much of what she taught in song, was a repetition of what she had learned in suffering.[14]

Looking for more from Elizabeth Prentiss?

---

[14] George Prentiss, The Life and Letters of Elizabeth Prentiss (Anson D. F. Randolph & Company 1882), 565-566

Check out our other books at MoreLoveEnterprises.com (or scan QR code below.) All books also available in e-book formats for iPad, Kindle, and Nook include color illustrations!

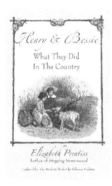

Henry and Bessie, What They Did in the Country (For ages 7-11)
Nidworth and His Three Magic Wands (For ages 12 to adult.)
Little Suzy's Six Birthdays (For ages 5-10)

Also...
Little Suzy's Little Helpers
Little Suzy's Six Teachers

...And more!